PRAISE FOR A

"Utterly unique and movingl
wonderful story about what hap
narrative, and find ways to communicate across the gaps in language.
Clever, brilliantly written, and thought-provoking, it will stay with you."
Sinéad O'Hart, author of *The Time Tider*

★

"It has been fantastic to read this novel. As someone who is a communication specialist and spends a lot of time helping children and young people to adapt and learn how they can better interact, this is a book that might go some way to helping the wider world understand the challenges those with selective mutism face and how we can better support them."
Eimear Monahan, Paediatric Speech and Language Therapist

PRAISE FOR *OUR SISTER, AGAIN*

"A beautiful exploration of grief, hope, and what it means to be human, Cameron weaves themes of ethics, AI, friendship and first love with a compelling mystery and bewitchingly-described Scottish location. This is an outstanding middle-grade debut from one of my favourite authors."
Simon James Green, author of *Life of Riley*

★

"I loved this book, it was perfect soft sci-fi
with very real themes of love and loss"
L. D. Lapinski, author of *The Strangeworlds Travel Agency*

★

"*Our Sister, Again* expertly weaves family drama with high concept sci-fi.
It's a captivating tale about AI written with real, human heart."
Annabelle Sami, author of *Llama Out Loud*

★

"A book about family, friendship, and what it means to be you.
One of those books you read in one day and think about forever."
Wibke Brueggemann, author of *Love is for Losers*

★

"A heart-warming and bittersweet examination of personhood, familial bonds and healing from loss"
Lauren James, author of *The Quiet at the End of the World*

★

"A powerful exploration of grief, technology and what makes us human, *Our Sister, Again* skilfully combines warm-hearted contemporary with a sci-fi twist to create a thought-provoking, thrilling read"
Lucy Powrie, author of *The Paper and Hearts Society*

★

"A truly remarkable story. Sad and life-affirming all at the same time. These characters are going to stay with me for a long time."
Lee Newbery, author of *The Last Firefox*

★

"*Our Sister, Again* is a rich, heartfelt story about family, grief, and what it means to be human told with immense gentleness and skill"
Ciara Smyth, author of *The Falling In Love Montage*

★

"An intriguing and tender portrayal of a life changing 'what if' – Sophie Cameron is a fabulous storyteller"
Polly Ho-Yen, author of *Boy In The Tower*

★

"*Our Sister, Again* is a vibrant exploration of love, personhood and everything in between. This is a book driven by a family's affection, for their daughter and their sister. Quietly thought-provoking, it'll have you questioning what it means to be human and how far someone will go for love."
Reads Rainbow blog

★

"A nuanced, moving exploration of grief and family, Cameron's deft prose and complex characters bring a wonderful new addition to LGBTQ+ fiction"
Kat Dunn, author of *Dangerous Remedy*

Away With Words

For Naïa – finally!

LITTLE TIGER
An imprint of Little Tiger Press Limited
1 Coda Studios, 189 Munster Road,
London SW6 6AW

Imported into the EEA by Penguin Random House Ireland, Morrison Chambers,
32 Nassau Street, Dublin D02 YH68

www.littletiger.co.uk

First published in Great Britain in 2023

ISBN: 978-1-78895-392-4

A CIP catalogue record for this book is available from the British Library.

Printed and bound in the UK.

The Forest Stewardship Council® (FSC®) is a global, not-for-profit organization dedicated to the promotion of responsible forest management worldwide. FSC defines standards based on agreed principles for responsible forest stewardship that are supported by environmental, social, and economic stakeholders. To learn more, visit www.fsc.org

2 4 6 8 10 9 7 5 3 1

Away With Words

Sophie Cameron

LITTLE TIGER
LONDON

One

The head teacher had *slugs* on his face. Lime–green, right in the middle of his chin.

Not the animal – the word.

The word slugs stuck to his chin in lime-green letters.

"Welcome ~~~~~~, Gala," Mr Watson said. "~~~~~~ ~~~~~~ school."

At least, that was how it sounded to me. I tried to read the missing words as they fell from the head teacher's mouth – they were bright and bold, egg-yolk yellow – but I was too distracted by the *slugs* on his face. Why had he been talking about slugs so early in the morning? Maybe he was a gardener and was worried about his vegetables. Maybe he stepped on one on his way into school and felt bad about it. Maybe he'd eaten them for breakfast. Maybe that was normal in Scotland.

Mr Watson must have noticed me staring because he brushed his hand over his chin, and the word *slugs* fell on to the desk. "I think you ~~~~~~ ~~~~~~," he told me. "~~~~~~ ~~~~~~ change, but ~~~~~~."

The sentence dropped

piece

by

piece

from Mr Watson's mouth and disappeared into the pile of words in front of him. It wasn't even nine o'clock yet, and his desk already looked like he'd spat out half a dictionary! I saw a few words I knew – a small grey *cold* caught behind the space bar on the keyboard, ***music*** in cursive purple letters by his coffee cup – but I still had no clue what he was saying.

Beside me, Papa smiled and nodded. "Gala is very ∿∿∿∿∿ ∿∿∿∿∿," he said, putting his hand on my shoulder. His voice slipped into that funny up-and-down thing it always did when he spoke English, as if his vocal cords were riding a carousel. "I am sure ∿∿∿∿∿ ∿∿∿∿∿ happy here."

The word happy caught on the collar of Papa's jacket. It was a light blue lie. I wasn't happy to be here. I didn't want to be in Scotland at all. It had only been five days since we'd moved here from Cadaqués, a little town by the sea in the north-east of Spain, but I already missed it so much it hurt. I wanted to be back at my old school, racing my friend Pau down the corridor and getting into trouble for talking too much in class. I wanted to go home.

As words spilled from the head teacher's mouth, there was a knock on the door. Mr Watson said a large orange, "Yes?", and two girls stepped into the office. They were both around my age, almost twelve. One was White and very tall with freckles and light brown hair, and the other was Black and short with smiley brown eyes and braces on her teeth. The tall one said something, and Mr Watson nodded.

"Thank you, ~~~~~~. Gala, this is ~~~~~~ and ~~~~~~," he said, turning back to me. "They ~~~~~~."

The girls smiled awkwardly at me as Mr Watson talked. There was a word he kept saying, something I'd never heard before. I realized from the way he was pointing to the girls that it was a name. When Papa nudged me to reply, I quickly scanned the desk and found it dangling from the tip of a pencil in Mr Watson's pen pot: *Eilidh.*

"Hello –" I tried to sound out the word – "Eyelid?"

The girls blinked at me, then the tall one's eyes went wide, and she said a lot of bright pink words very, very quickly.

Seeing I was lost, Papa finally switched to Catalan, the language we spoke at home. It turned out *Eilidh* was their name – both of them, Eilidh Chisholm and Eilidh Obiaka – and it was pronounced 'A-lee'.

Mr Watson and Papa both chuckled at my mistake, and the girls giggled too. It wasn't a mean sort of laughter, but I felt my cheeks go red. Why bother spelling it E-I-L-I-D-H if they weren't going to pronounce half the letters? That made no sense whatsoever.

Outside Mr Watson's office, a bell rang. He and Papa stood up and moved towards the door, so I did the same. From the way the Eilidhs lingered by the doorway, I guessed they were here to show me to my first class. The one with braces, Eilidh O, gave me another smile and stepped aside to let me into the corridor.

It was noisy now, dozens of kids laughing or swinging their bags or shoving last-minute breakfasts into their mouths as they went to their classes. This place was bigger than my last school, and with everyone rushing around it felt enormous – there must have been twice as many kids here. But that wasn't the reason my mouth fell open.

It was because of the words.

Hundreds and thousands of words falling out of mouths

and flying through the air,

bouncing off

walls

and

fluttering

to

the

floor.

ANGRY RED WORDS and happy yellow ones. *Timid whispers in pastel tones* and **excited shouts in bold, thick fonts**. There were tired words that **blurred with a yawn around the edges**, and *sleek cursive words that could only have come from rumours and secrets.* There were so many that they already came up past my ankles – a glittering stream of speech curving past the reception desk and along the corridor as kids splashed through it without a second thought.

My old school was filled with words too. Back there, I never paid them much attention. Sometimes my friends and I would flick them across the desk to each other when we were bored in class, but I'd never thought about how many there were around us. Not even when the school cleaners came to sweep them all away at the end of the day. When I was speaking Catalan or Spanish, I hardly noticed when the words left my mouth – I just brushed them off my clothes or picked them away if they landed in my food. Here they were all I could see, all I could hear. And I could barely understand anything.

"Are you OK, bug?" Papa asked me in Catalan. "I know it's a lot but you'll get used to it."

Seeing words in our own language and Papa's familiar ochre shades felt like a lifebelt, but it was quickly pulled away when Mr Watson said a loud white, "Oh!" He went to reception, spoke to the woman standing behind the desk and came back holding a sheet of paper.

"Your 〰〰〰, Gala," he said, handing it to me. "Eilidh and Eilidh will 〰〰〰."

On the paper was a timetable with Class 1C at the top and my subjects printed below. When I looked up,

Mr Watson was pointing towards the corridor behind reception, but I couldn't catch what he was saying. There were too many words whirling round us, and I couldn't pick out the ones I needed. Papa explained in Catalan that the Eilidhs were in most of my classes, and they would show me to registration. I didn't even know what 'registration' meant. It sounded like it might be something to do with computers or filing cabinets.

"OK, Gala?" Papa touched my hair and smiled. "Have fun. I'll see you at home."

Papa shook Mr Watson's hand, said a bright blue goodbye to the Eilidhs, then waved to me again before walking towards the main doors. Ever since we arrived in Scotland last week, all the English words that I'd learned at my old school and from Papa and TV shows had been jumbled up in my head, a puzzle that I couldn't put together. But, as I followed the two Eilidhs towards the next classroom, a few pieces finally connected.

This is NOT my home.

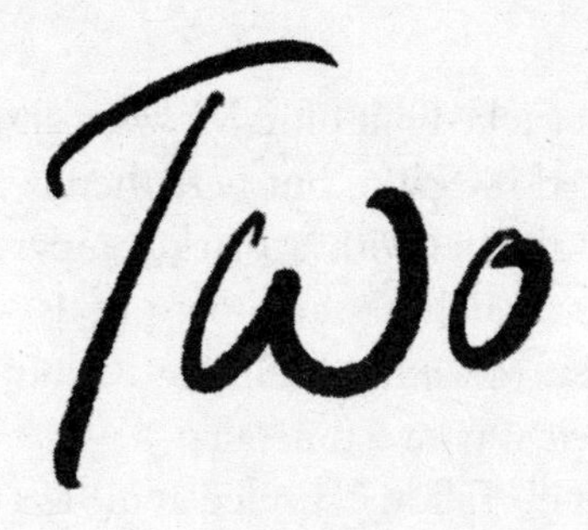

Before Papa and I moved here, I looked up the distance between Fortrose and Cadaqués on his tablet. It said 1,105 miles as the crow flies, which is 1,778 kilometres. Now we were here, it seemed like even more. Fortrose was a small town by the sea, just like Cadaqués, but *everything* else about it was different. Our town was all white buildings that sparkled in the sunshine, boats that bobbed on the water as I cycled along the promenade. It was playing football with my friends on the beach and the place on the corner that made the world's best churros.

There were no churros in Fortrose and not much sunshine, either. Even so, when we first came to visit last August, I liked it a lot. I liked how green everything was, and the swirly ice creams with a stick of flaky chocolate on top that Ryan bought us from the beach café near his house. It wasn't the sort of summer I was used to, but I didn't mind – it was nice to have a break from the sticky hot weather, the mosquitoes, the streets filled with tourists.

But now it was January, and everything was *dull.* The buildings were brown or beige. The days were short and cold and grey. Even this school looked like all the colour had been sucked out of it. We were allowed to wear whatever we liked in Spain, but here there was a uniform – a white shirt and tie with a black jumper and a black skirt or trousers. Watching the other pupils walk through the corridors that morning, I felt like I'd joined a gang of penguins on their way to a funeral.

"〰〰〰 first!" Eilidh C smiled at me as I followed her through the crowd of students. Her words were bubblegum pink with smooth lines that flicked out at the edges. "〰〰〰 Music."

"It's 〰〰〰 favourite," Eilidh O added, smiling. Her words were smaller than Eilidh C's, more delicate, but their letters were lemon yellow. "Do you 〰〰〰 〰〰〰?"

They both spoke too fast for me to read everything they were saying, and the chatter around us made it even harder to hear. Seeing I wasn't following, Eilidh O pointed to the timetable that Mr Watson had given me. There were seven classes a day. Today started with Geography, then Music. So … they were saying that we had Geography first, and Music was their favourite?

Normally I would have lots to say about that. I could mention that I knew how to play a bit of guitar and piano. I'd tell them about my favourite bands and ask about theirs too. But I couldn't find the words for any of that in English.

"OK," I said instead. Two letters, muddy brown, and I wasn't sure they made sense, seeing as I didn't know what the question was. Still, it was the only word I'd spoken since I arrived except 'hello' and 'eyelid' (and I couldn't even remember what that last one meant).

The Eilidhs led me into a classroom at the end of the

corridor. Some kids gave me curious looks as I walked in, but most were talking or scrolling through their phones, and others were just Monday-morning sleepy. Leaning back against a wooden desk was a woman with curly red hair and very large glasses. Eilidh C went up to her and spoke in excited orange. I caught my name, even though she pronounced my surname wrong, and the word 'Spain'.

"Oh wow!" The teacher smiled at me and said something about 'lovely' (or maybe it was 'lucky') and told me that her name was Ms Anderson.

That was another thing that was different – instead of calling teachers by their first names, the kids had to say Ms This or Mr That, as if they were in one of the old-fashioned TV shows that Iaia, my grandmother, liked so much.

"Remember," Papa had said to me that morning, "when you see Ryan at school, you call him Mr Young, OK?"

Ryan – or 'Mr Young' – was a PE teacher here. He was also Papa's boyfriend and the reason we moved to Fortrose. He used to visit us during the holidays, and Papa would go to Scotland once a month while I stayed with Iaia. But after two years Papa and Ryan decided they wanted to live together all the time. They also decided they had to do that in Fortrose, which meant I was forced to leave my friends and my school and our town and our flat and move here with Papa.

I didn't get to decide anything.

So now I was here, squeezing into an empty desk behind the two Eilidhs instead of yawning through my Spanish literature class. Gazing round the room, I spotted a few kids staring at me. Two girls whispered slick silvery words to each other behind their hands until they saw me watching and turned away, both giggling. A strange, lonely feeling filled my chest. It made me miss home even more.

As the last few kids trailed into the classroom, Ms Anderson sat down at her desk. She said a lot of pale green words I couldn't catch, then turned to her computer. "Ross Amos?"

A red-haired boy raised one lazy hand in the air. "Here, miss."

She called Eilidh C next, and then a girl called Caitlin Douglas. So registration was like a roll-call. My surname was Vilanova, so I knew I'd be near the end of the list. My hands went clammy as I waited for my turn to speak, but when she got to me Ms Anderson looked up and smiled instead.

"We have ~~~~~~ ~~~~~~ ~~~~~~ today. ~~~~~~ ~~~~~~ Gala Vilanova, ~~~~~~ ~~~~~~ ~~~~~~ Spain. Would ~~~~~~ ~~~~~~ ~~~~~~, Gala?"

Every single face in the class turned to look at me. Eilidh O smiled, and the classroom light caught the metal of her braces, making her mouth sparkle. I gave a wobbly smile back and took a deep breath. I had to say something, and I knew Ms Anderson had asked a question from the way her voice went up at the end of the sentence.

"Hello," I eventually croaked. Normally my words were quite shiny, with chunky lines and sharp corners, but this one came out watery blue and smudged around the edges, as if I'd borrowed someone else's voice. I didn't like it, so I tried again. "Hello."

There was a pause, and then the boy behind me sniggered

before Ms Anderson shushed him. My cheeks went hot again. Had I said something wrong? Eilidh C leaned over the back of her chair and spoke very slowly. I managed to read some of the words as they fell from her mouth:

wants,

tell,

about.

Ms Anderson wanted me to tell them something about myself? I'd go with that.

"My name is Gala," I said awkwardly. "I have eleven years. I am Spain."

This time two more people laughed. The teacher said something to them in sharp green, then looked at me and said, "Sorry, Gala."

My eyes were stinging but I was more annoyed than upset – at the kids who laughed at me and also at myself. At my old school, English was one of my best subjects. I got full marks on the test we did just before Christmas! But, like everything else, it was different here. People talked like they were running out of words, and their accents weren't like the ones in the videos we watched in class for practice.

A few of the words that I'd spoken had stuck on my black jumper, so I brushed them on to the desk and tried to work out what I'd got wrong. It eventually clicked: I'd forgotten the word 'from' before 'Spain' and it was 'I *am* eleven', not 'I have eleven'. I tried to correct myself, but the words became tangled in my mouth, and I had to swallow them back down. By then, Ms Anderson had finished checking attendance and the moment had gone.

I turned to look through the window so no one would notice my glossy eyes. Outside, it was starting to rain over the quiet grey courtyard. There were no table-tennis tables like we had at my old school, just one lonely basketball hoop on the opposite wall. Even the courtyard couldn't compare to the one back home.

I remembered something that Iaia had said when I spoke to her the night before. She'd told me to make a list of everything that I liked best about each place, so that I could concentrate on the good parts of my new life and look forward to things when I went home to visit her at Easter. She'd been trying to make me feel better about moving here, but I didn't *want* to feel better about it. I wanted to sulk. And, after being made to move 1,778 kilometres, I *deserved* to sulk. So, taking a pen from my bag, I wrote my list in tiny letters on the back of my timetable.

The best things about:

Fortrose	Cadaqués
NOTHING!!!	Everything.

And that, I thought to myself, was never going to change.

Three

When somebody talks a lot, Iaia always says they 'chat more than a parakeet'. That's exactly what the Eilidhs were like. They spoke non-stop as we walked from registration to our first class, their words twirling round each other as they fell to the ground. Eilidh O had started to talk to me more slowly, though, so I was able to read some of what she was saying. That was how I learned that she and Eilidh C both lived in a village a few miles away from here, and that they had been best friends for five years. (Or maybe it was since they were five years old. Either way, it was a long time. Almost as long as Pau and me.)

When we reached the Geography classroom, Eilidh C pointed to a desk in the front row. "We ~~~~~~ here," she told me, putting her bag on top of it.

She hurried up to the teacher's desk, where a bald man in a red jumper was stifling a yawn. He nodded and gave me a tired smile as Eilidh C explained who I was. The timetable said his name was Mr Menzies, and that was the word that came out of his mouth when he introduced himself, but the way he said it sounded like 'Ming-iss'. That made even less sense than Eilidh sounding like 'A-lee'!

Mr Menzies pointed to a desk beside the one where the Eilidhs had left their bags. As soon as I sat down, Eilidh O said something and spun round, holding a pencil case shaped like a milk carton. Inside were lots of pens and pencils decorated with cartoon characters. My hand hovered as I wondered if she'd asked if I wanted to borrow one. Eilidh nodded and nudged the case forward, so I took a pen with a cute plastic dog on the top of it. When I pressed it down, the nib of the pen changed colour from red to blue to green.

"Thank you," I said. I had my own stationery, but nothing as nice as hers.

Eilidh O leaned over the gap between the desks and pointed to the dog. "~~~~~~ 'dog' in Spanish?" she asked, her words coming out in clear teal letters.

I wanted to tell her that my main language was Catalan. I learned Spanish in school and spoke it with some of my friends, and I watched lots of films and TV series in it, but Catalan was what I spoke at home with Papa and with Iaia. But I didn't know how to explain all of that, so I just answered the question.

"*Perro,*" I said. "Dog is *perro.*"

"*Perro,*" Eilidh O repeated, but she had trouble with the double r and it came out wrong.

I said it a second time, exaggerating the sound. Eilidh tried again and again. Eilidh C joined in too, and then a few other kids around us. Soon the desks and floor were cluttered with *perrrrro*, *perrrrrrrrro*, *perrrrrrrrrrrro*, almost like little sausage dogs, each longer than the last. It all looked and sounded so silly that I forgot that I was supposed to be in a bad mood and started giggling.

perrrrro

perrrrrrrrrro

perrrro *perro* *perrro* *perr*

"OK, that's enough," said Mr Menzies. ('Enough' was another weird word – why did that gh sound like an f?) He went to the whiteboard and wrote something. "Mountains," he read out, with a yawn so big that we could see the fillings in his back teeth.

A cloud rolled over my brief spot of happiness as soon as he started the lesson. Mr Menzies spoke in a low grey mumble that slid from his mouth like dirty water running from a tap, so fast I couldn't even tell where one word ended and the next began. When he handed out a worksheet for us to label all the different parts of a mountain, I felt more lost than if he'd sent me off to climb one without a map.

"Here." Eilidh C leaned to the right so I could see her worksheet on the desk in front of me. She said something I couldn't catch, but I could tell from her grin and the warm shades of the words that she meant for me to copy. I wrote down the answers as quickly as I could, not bothering to stop and check the spelling.

"Thank you," I whispered. That brought my word count for the whole lesson up to seven. The teachers back home who wrote *Gala is a clever girl but talks too much in class!* on my report cards would never have believed it.

When the bell rang, I packed up my stuff and followed the Eilidhs to the next classroom. At my old school, each class had their own room, and the teachers came to us, but here there were separate rooms for each subject, and we had to move between them. Music was at the other end of the building and, by the time we got there, there were words stuck all over my shoes and trousers.

Luckily this class was easier: I didn't need words to play a song on a keyboard, or to laugh along when a boy called

Ross started singing in a loud voice that sounded just like the seagulls cawing outside.

Even so, by the time the bell rang for break, I was really tired and having trouble taking much in. The Eilidhs were still chattering over each other, and by now the current of words running through the corridors came all the way up to my calves. The girls went upstairs and joined a group of kids sitting in a circle in the corridor. They introduced themselves as **Scott**, *Olu*, Frankie and *Amina*. Their names and greetings fell to the floor like confetti, each one in their own personal style and a different colour.

"This is Gala," Eilidh C said. She was starting to feel like my own personal introducer, if there was such a thing. "She's ∼∼∼∼∼∼ ∼∼∼∼∼∼ ∼∼∼∼∼∼ Spain."

The girl called Amina said something, but I didn't understand what. Everyone was talking so fast, words flying here and there as they shoved crisps and snacks into their mouths. I took out the sandwich and the clementines that Papa had packed in my bag and tried to keep up.

Olu used a translation app on her phone to ask me a bunch of questions, including if it was true that I lived with Mr Young. I nodded and said yes, that he was my dad's boyfriend. Ryan and Papa had been worried that kids would tease me about that, but everyone smiled. Clearly they all liked Ryan. I used to like him too, until he made me move away from my friends and Iaia and everything I knew.

"∼∼∼∼∼∼ that?"

The boy called Scott was looking at my sandwich. I opened the bread to show the small bar of chocolate inside. Everyone's eyes went wide.

"A chocolate sandwich?" Olu said loudly. "That's so ~~~~~~!"

Eilidh C's nose had wrinkled up like I'd revealed a sandwich full of slugs. I didn't get it. It was no different from Nutella on toast, and I knew people here ate that because Ryan had it all the time. Not everyone seemed to find it strange, though. Frankie called it 'amazing', and Eilidh O said something in a warm apricot colour. She pointed to the sandwich, then mimed making one for herself. I smiled, ripped off the end of mine and passed it to her. Everyone waited for her verdict as she chewed.

"~~~~~~ good!"

I wanted to tell her that I would bring her one the next day but I spent too long searching for the words and missed my chance. Eilidh C offered me some of her crisps, and Amina used the app to ask me a few more questions. Scott showed me a photo of the town in Spain where he went on holiday last year, then they all got caught up arguing about something with Frankie, and I lost track.

Soon I gave up trying to follow and just sat and ate the clementines that Papa had packed for me, wondering what my friends back home were doing. They'd be in Biology: Pau would probably be on his third warning for talking too much, and Laia and Mariam would no doubt be in a fit of giggles over nothing. The time difference meant they were always an hour ahead of me now. Like they were in the future, and I could never catch up.

Ten minutes later, the bell rang for the next class. The Eilidhs had French but I was going to have one-on-one English lessons to help me learn faster. Amina and Frankie showed me where the classroom was so I didn't get lost.

As I walked down the corridor, I heard someone call my name. Ryan was jogging towards me, words splashing round him with every step.

"Gala, ∼∼∼∼∼∼ for you! ∼∼∼∼∼∼ first day?"

I shrugged. "Is OK."

"That's great. ∼∼∼∼∼∼ ∼∼∼∼∼∼ anything, OK?" Ryan smiled. When I didn't answer, he squeezed my shoulder. "Well, I'm ∼∼∼∼∼∼ if ∼∼∼∼∼∼ ∼∼∼∼∼∼ me. See you at home."

The word *home* fell past his hoodie and on to the floor. I wanted to stamp on it with my shiny new black shoes. Home for me and Papa was Cadaqués. It was our small, cosy flat with the pink and purple flowers that grew all over the balcony. It was the squashy old sofa in the living room and the little green parrots that woke me up singing outside my window. It was not this cold grey country. It was not quiet, sleepy Fortrose. And it was *definitely* not Ryan's house.

"This is not my home," I said in jerky red letters, just like I'd imagined telling Papa earlier that morning. I switched to loud, angry Catalan. "I wish we'd never come here. I'm going to make Papa move back, with or without you."

After a whole morning of English, it felt really good to speak normally, without having to move the words around like building blocks inside my head. Ryan's eyes flicked from right to left and up and down, just like mine had been doing all morning – he was trying to read what I'd said. He crouched down until his face was level with mine.

"Gala, I know it is difficult," he said in very slow, strange Catalan. He'd started learning a year ago but his words still came out spelled wrong or with letters missing.

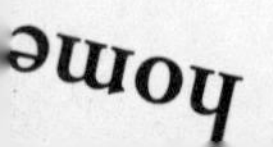

Sometimes I couldn't understand it at all. He rubbed his forehead. "Argh, what's the word for ~~~~~~? It is…"

Finally someone was speaking my language, or at least trying to, but I didn't want to hear it. I turned round so sharply that my bag bumped against Ryan, and I stormed towards the learning-support classroom. Ryan called after me a couple of times, which made a few kids waiting outside other classes look round curiously. Guilt started to creep up on me as I stomped through the river of words filling the corridor, but I didn't look back.

Then, as I turned the corner, I saw something that made me stop.

Crouching by the staircase was a girl around my age. She was White and very pale with lots of frizzy blond hair. She had one hand inside her open schoolbag, like she was trying to find an item she needed, but it was clear from the way her eyes darted about that she was up to something. Taking a step behind the wall so she couldn't see me, I watched as she reached into the pile of words by the bottom step. The girl took one last look around, then picked up a word with her thumb and index finger and slid it into her jacket pocket.

My stomach flipped. I had seen people push others' old words away or even sift through them if they were trying to find something they'd said, but I'd never seen anyone *take* another person's word before. It seemed so strange to me … as if the girl was picking up a piece of someone's personality and keeping it for herself.

But maybe that was yet another thing that was different here in Fortrose.

I was exaggerating when I said there was absolutely nothing I liked about Fortrose. There were two things, and they came bounding towards me when I opened the door to Ryan's house that afternoon: Celine, a fluffy black Pomeranian who thought she was the toughest dog on earth, and Dion, a dopey Great Dane who loved biscuits and cuddles. Dion leaped up and pushed me on to the carpet while Celine began nipping at my school trousers.

"Celine, stop!" I laughed. I spoke in Catalan and the words came out the colour of candyfloss. "Those are new!"

Papa kept telling me Celine and Dion only understood English, but I was sure they were superdogs who knew every language in the world. Besides, it didn't matter how I spoke to them – Celine never listened to a word anyone said, including Ryan, and right now Dion just wanted to lick my face. I laughed and tried to push him away as he started slobbering all over me, then stopped when I heard footsteps coming from the kitchen. I didn't want Papa to think that my first day had gone well.

His expression was anxious as he stepped into the hallway. "How did it go?" he asked in hopeful yellow.

"Bad," I said, big and bold and grey. "I hate the uniform, they don't have ping-pong tables outside, and I couldn't understand *anything*."

Papa's face fell, but just for a moment. "I'm sorry, bug. But it was only your first day. It's normal that things feel strange at first."

Ryan was outside chatting with one of the neighbours. He'd caught up with me after I left school, and we'd walked the last few minutes to his house together. He kept asking me questions about how my day had gone, then asking even more questions when I gave one-word answers to the first ones. If he was annoyed at me for shouting at him earlier, he didn't show it. He didn't tell Papa about it when he came inside, either. Instead he said something about me making friends.

"Nice ~~~~~~ of kids," he said as he looked through the letters that Papa had placed for him on the table in the hallway.

I scowled up at him from the floor but Papa's worried expression turned into a big smile. "That's great," he said, switching to English. "See? I knew you ~~~~~~ have no ~~~~~~."

"They're not my friends," I snapped in Catalan as Dion rolled over to have his giant belly petted. "Pau and Laia and Mariam – remember them? The people I'll probably never see ever again because you made me move thousands of kilometres away? *They* are my friends. If they haven't already forgotten about me, that is."

"How could anyone forget about you, Drama Queen?" Papa prodded my side with his toe and smiled. When I didn't return it, he added, "Let's take the dogs for a walk before it gets too dark. Maybe we'll see these dolphins that Ryan is always talking about."

Celine started leaping and barking at the sound of the word 'walk' – I *knew* she could understand Catalan. Ryan told us to go ahead without him, or something like that, so Papa went to get the dogs' leashes and his big black coat, gloves and two scarves. Even if he wouldn't admit it, he was obviously having trouble getting used to the Scottish winter.

The sun had already set when we left, even though it was only just gone four o'clock. Papa took out the torch he'd brought with him, and we walked along the coastal path lining the golf course and towards what Ryan called the Point, a long, thin strip of land with a lighthouse at the tip. Papa had spent the whole day job-hunting online, and he told me about some of the weirder offers. There was even a zoo looking for a penguin trainer.

"You should apply!" I started waddling like a penguin. "I could drop out of school and help."

"No, thank you, Gala. I don't think I'm qualified for the job." Papa laughed. "I'll have to just keep looking."

"Why doesn't Ryan look for a job in Spain instead?" I asked. "That way we could all go home."

Papa let out a long sigh and ran a hand through his hair. He had exactly the same hair as me, dark brown and shiny. "We've talked about this, bug," he said. "Ryan wouldn't be able to get a job there. Not as a PE teacher anyway. He doesn't speak the language well enough yet."

"He could learn," I said in a surly green. "Just like you're making *me* learn."

"He's trying," Papa said, which was true – Ryan was

always tapping away on the language-learning apps on his phone. "But it would take him years to get up to the level he'd need to work there. It's much easier for kids than it is for adults."

It didn't seem very easy for kids. Before we left, everyone had kept saying that once I was here I'd soak up the language like a sponge. So far I felt more like a stone, having buckets and buckets of words thrown over me without any of them seeping in.

"Why can't things just be like they used to?" I asked. My words were coming out stretched in the middle, the way they always did when I was whining. "He lives here, and we live there, and you just visit each other."

"It got too difficult. Too much travelling back and forth. It was tiring, and expensive, and we missed each other. Besides, he's part of the family now."

"No, he's not." The words came out tiny and so faint they were almost transparent, but Papa still spotted them.

"Yes, he is, Gala." When I didn't answer, he put his arm round me. "Come on, what's this about? I know you like Ryan."

He poked me in the ribs until my frown turned into a reluctant laugh. Deep down, I did like Ryan. It was hard not to: he was always in a good mood, almost always smiling and making jokes. I used to love it when he came to visit us in Cadaqués. We'd always do fun things, like go snorkelling or on day trips to Barcelona. Back then, he spoke no Catalan or Spanish at all, but it didn't seem to matter much. We didn't need to talk to play games or go swimming or go out for ice cream. Last summer he stayed with us for a whole month before we came to Fortrose for the second half of the holidays, and it was great – Papa laughed and smiled so much when Ryan was around, and I liked having him there too.

But now it was his fault we were *here*.

"I shouted at him today," I told Papa. The words were small and flushed pink with guilt. "At school."

"You did?" There was a flash of anger in Papa's eyes, but then he took a deep breath and looked towards the sea. "That's not fair, Gala."

"Well, it's not fair I had to leave." I kicked at a stone and watched it bounce across the beach. "I want to go home."

"We'll visit soon." His rust-coloured words shone in the beam of the torch. They were hardening around the edges now, the way they always did when he was starting to get annoyed. "The time's going to fly by, I promise."

Papa had already booked tickets for all three of us to go back to Cadaqués in the Easter holidays. That was over three months away. It seemed like forever but at least it gave me three months to change his mind. That would be more than enough time to convince him that I really was miserable here. And moving back was definitely a possibility because we still had our old flat. Papa had put it on the market months ago but he hadn't been able to find a buyer, so in the end we moved over here with the stuff we needed and left the rest. If I tried hard enough, I could be back in my old life before summer.

We turned past the lighthouse and came to the sandy part of the beach. I'd come here for a walk with Papa and Ryan when we visited Fortrose in August. Back then, there were lots of people standing around, hoping to spot the dolphins that apparently swam in the area, but they hadn't appeared.

It was too dark to see them now, even if they did decide to show up. Dion went bounding into the water, and Celine raced towards the grassy banks to sniff around. The wind was quite strong, and it sent our words flying out to sea as soon as they left our mouths. As the torchlight swept over the ground, I saw there were others mixed in with the sand blowing over my feet. One, seagull, got caught on the laces of my trainers for a few seconds before it broke free and flitted towards the grass.

"Do people pick up words here?" I asked Papa.

He turned to look at me. "What do you mean?"

I pointed to the words fluttering over our shoes. Most were in English but a few were in other languages or alphabets I didn't understand. I knelt and picked one up – **encourage** in curved royal blue letters.

"Like this."

An odd feeling came over me as I held it up to show Papa. I'd touched other people's words before – sometimes you had to if they were creating too much clutter, and you had to push them out of the way – but holding one between my thumb and finger felt much stranger.

"Not that I know of," Papa said, frowning. "Why?"

"I saw a girl picking them up at school. She was putting them in her pocket. Like she was keeping them."

"Oh. Really? I've heard of people saving words before, but I don't think it's common here." He looked at the word I was holding. "Do you know what this one means? It means to give someone hope or confidence. *Animar* in Catalan."

"Encourage," I read.

Papa made me repeat it a few more times until the word looked and sounded just right, then broke off when we heard a loud bark from further up the beach – Celine was trying to pick a fight with a Labrador and its owner. As Papa ran off to apologize and wrangle Celine away, I looked at the word again: **encourage**, flat against my palm like a tattoo.

All spoken words faded eventually. Most of them vanished after a few days, but more powerful or heartfelt ones could stick around for weeks or even months. This one probably had a day to go before it disappeared altogether – I could tell from its faint colour and soft edges. Even so, the feeling from the word grew the longer I held it, as if the speaker's emotion still lived in the letters. It felt like hope, with a tingling of fear.

"Encourage," I read again, putting the stress on the second syllable like Papa had told me. I let the word fly away on the breeze, but the hopeful feeling still tickled at my skin as I ran across the sand to join him.

encourage

Five

Somehow the next couple of days at school were even harder than that first Monday. I didn't understand a single word Mr Calvin said in History. I got the labels on the containers mixed up in Home Economics and added salt to my cake instead of sugar. When Frankie asked me which TV shows I liked at break time, I got so tongue-tied that the words came out looking like a keyboard smash. If learning was a ladder, I had fallen off the first rung and was back on the floor.

I kept thinking about Harry Rooney. He was a boy in my old class who moved to Cadaqués from England when we were nine. There were quite a few kids in my school from the UK, Ireland, the US… I'd never thought about how hard it must have been for them to be thrown into a class when they didn't know any Catalan or Spanish, especially when lots of people there flipped between the two languages every few sentences.

But it wasn't the *same*. There were always some teachers who could speak English to help them out, and the rest of us had learned enough to at least be able to say hello and ask their names. And if they found it too difficult, which a few of them did, sometimes their parents sent them to English-speaking international schools instead. There were no options like that for me here.

My one-to-one lessons helped a bit. They were with a teacher called Miss Shah who had lots of curly black hair and liked to wear earrings shaped like colourful birds. We would read simple books and go over vocabulary and pronunciation together, but there were so many things about English that didn't make sense. If *through* sounded like *threw*, then why didn't *dough* sound like *dew*? Why did they say an alarm went off when it actually turned on? And those plurals – sometimes they added an s, and sometimes the word stayed the same, and sometimes it changed completely!

"It's just the way it is," Miss Shah told me.

She was much easier to understand than most people here. Her voice was very clear, and her words came out in large, neat letters that made them easy for me to read. So far she was definitely my favourite teacher.

"I am –" I searched for the right word on the list of states and emotions that we were studying – "exhausted."

Miss Shah's toucan earrings jingled as she laughed. "Yes, I can imagine. But soon it will be ~~~~~~."

She pointed at the word that had fallen on to the desk: *easy*. I scrunched up my mouth in a doubtful expression. I'd had a few moments over the past two days when I could understand whole sentences, and it seemed like Miss Shah was right, that things were getting better. But most of the time it felt like the current of words that flowed through the school was rising up, up, up into a tidal wave, waiting to pull me under and drown me in nouns and verbs and adjectives.

Luckily I had Maths after lunch. That was my favourite subject back home and the only one I'd been looking forward to here. Unless Scotland had some strange system Papa and Ryan hadn't warned me about, numbers would be exactly the same here as they were everywhere else.

Eilidh C wasn't in my class for this subject but Eilidh O was, so she persuaded the teacher to let her swap places with a boy called Michael so we could sit together. She offered to let me borrow something from her milk-carton pencil case again. This time I picked a mechanical pencil covered with drawings of cats.

"Good ∼∼∼∼∼∼. I love cats," Eilidh O said. "I have two, and three ∼∼∼∼∼∼."

She whipped out her phone and opened her gallery. On the screen was a picture of two cats and three guinea pigs, all lined up on a squashy red sofa. Neither of the cats looked very happy about the situation.

"This is Pom-Pom, Cookie and Bao," Eilidh said, pointing to the guinea pigs. I read the names as they fell. Each one came out a different colour, so they looked like little bits of rainbow on the desk. "And Whiskers and Stitch."

They were really cute, especially Cookie, who had brown-and-white fur that stuck out in a dozen different directions. I'd never had a pet of my own – Papa always said our flat back in Cadaqués was too small – but I had lots of pictures of Celine and Dion on my phone. When I showed them to Eilidh O, she gasped and clapped her hands together.

"Mr Young's dogs! He's shown us photos of them

~~~~~~ times. They're so cute," she said. "I wish he ~~~~~~ bring them to school."

That made me smile, partly because I was happy that I'd managed to understand almost every word that Eilidh had said, and partly because the idea of the dogs coming to school was quite funny. I pictured Celine chasing kids down the corridors, yapping at their ankles, and Dion bounding into classrooms and leaping on to desks to give out his big, slobbery hugs.

I wanted to describe the scene to Eilidh, but it took me so long to try to put together the sentences in my head that the silence started to get awkward. Eilidh quickly filled the gap by showing me what they'd done in Maths last week to catch me up. By the time she finished, it was too late for me to start talking about the dogs again.

Our Maths teacher, a man called Mr Henderson with a scratchy black beard a bit like Papa's, came over to our desk. He pointed to Eilidh O's textbook and asked me a question, so I guessed he wanted to know if I had one of my own. I shook my head. He said something to the class, gave everyone a look like he was shooting lasers out of his eyes, then walked towards the door. As it slammed shut behind him, I noticed a shock of frizzy blond hair in the front row. It belonged to the girl I'd seen picking up words on Monday.

Everyone else had started talking the second Mr Henderson left, but the girl just opened her book and began working. Behind her, a dark-haired boy and a girl with a long mousy ponytail were whispering together. The boy's words fell to the floor but the girl caught hers and smashed them in her hands so no one could see them.
~~~~~~

From the bitter colour that stained her palms, I guessed they weren't very nice.

"Hey, Natalie?" The boy leaned forward. "Are you ~~~~~~ ~~~~~~?"

Some people laughed. The girl called Natalie didn't react. Apart from a tiny twitch of her shoulders, it was like she hadn't heard him at all.

"She's ~~~~~~," the girl with the ponytail said. "~~~~~~ ~~~~~~ you?"

More people laughed this time, though not Eilidh O and not me. Some of the laughter was a bit half-hearted, like people were pushing themselves to join in, but some of it was loud and just plain mean.

"That's Craig and Abigail," Eilidh O whispered. "They're ~~~~~~."

I wanted to tell them to shut up and leave the word girl alone, but the words caught in my throat. What if I'd got it wrong, and they were just laughing with her, not at her? This might be some in-joke that I wasn't able to follow yet. But I could tell from the way that Natalie's hands curled into fists and how she leaned closer to her work that she didn't find it funny. Whatever they were saying, it was nasty.

The teacher came back and gave another death-ray stare to get everyone to stop chatting. I couldn't follow much of his talk on algebra, but I finished the exercises in the book before anyone else in the class – it was stuff I'd already covered back home. Mr Henderson ticked off all my answers and gave me a thumbs up, which put a big smile on my face. After floundering in strange words all week, numbers felt like finding dry land.

When we left the classroom, I had a question ready for Eilidh O. Eilidh C was waiting for us in the corridor, so I pushed the words out quickly before she started chattering and I missed my chance.

"Who is this girl with the blond hair?"

I'd been shaping the words in my head since I'd finished my classwork, making sure I'd get them right, and they came out in clear sky-blue letters. Eilidh C's eyebrows rose in surprise, and Eilidh O beamed. It was the longest sentence I'd spoken all week.

"Which girl?" Eilidh C asked.

I pointed to Natalie. She'd left the classroom quickly and was already halfway down the corridor. Eilidh C told me her name was Natalie Napier, then said something to do with 'speak'. When she saw I was trying to read what she'd said, she put her finger to her lips and shook her head. Eilidh O added something then, frowning slightly, and they both spoke too quickly for me to understand. Finally Eilidh C turned back to me.

"Natalie is –" her nose wrinkled, just like it had when she'd seen my chocolate sandwich on Monday – "a bit weird."

Weird. I knew that word. It wasn't always a bad thing, but from the way it came out of Eilidh C's mouth – a sour lime colour – she didn't mean it in a good way.

"She's not weird. She's just very quiet." Eilidh O made her words small and silvery, though Natalie was too far away to hear us. "I don't think I've ∼∼∼∼∼ heard her speak."

Eilidh C said something that I couldn't catch and laughed. She changed the subject to the French test she and Eilidh O had after lunch, but that lime-green ***weird*** loomed in my head all through break. I wondered if people here thought I was weird. I didn't speak much, either, and I ate things like chocolate sandwiches. Maybe one day everyone would be laughing at *me*.

Friday began with school assembly, where Mr Watson spent half an hour talking about things like uniform rules and recycling, and ended with a lesson on *A Midsummer Night's Dream* in double English. The class was completely impossible, even with Miss Shah there to help me, but I felt a bit better when I realized no one else seemed to know what this Shakespeare guy was going on about, either.

By the time the last bell rang that afternoon, I was exhausted. It had been a very long, very tiring week. Part of me just wanted to go back to Ryan's, curl up in bed and sleep all weekend.

Another bigger part of me just wanted to *talk*. There were so many thoughts and opinions and jokes that I'd had to push down because I didn't have the words for them and, over the weekend, they came bursting out of me in a thousand different colours. It was such a relief to be able to speak my own language again, to see the words coming fast and fully formed from my mouth. I could have talked until they filled up the entire house, bursting through the doors and flying out of the chimney like fireworks.

Apart from asking me to read out the instructions for

the desk that he and Ryan were building for my room, Papa didn't push me to speak English that Saturday. He could see that I needed a break, and he let me have it – until after lunch on Sunday, when Ryan suggested we play a card game called Dobble.

"Let's make a rule," Papa said. "English only."

I pulled the cards towards me. They were decorated with illustrations of all sorts of objects: trees and moons, ghosts and stop signs. "No. That's too hard."

"We'll go over the words first. I bet you know most of them already." Papa pointed to a skull and crossbones and switched to English. "What is this called?"

I shrugged. "A … dead head?"

Ryan laughed. "It's called a skull," he said, the word falling to the table in pumpkin orange. "But 'dead head' works too."

I started dealing out the cards, hoping Papa would forget about his English-only rule, but he made me learn lots of random words like 'padlock' and 'shamrock' before we even started. I lost the first four rounds because it took me too long to remember the names of the items, even though Ryan was moving at a glacier pace in an obvious attempt to let me win, and Papa kept correcting me whenever I got the pronunciation wrong. I was starting to feel really stressed. I'd had five whole days of this at school; I didn't want Ryan's house to feel like another classroom. Eventually I gave up and threw all my cards on to the table.

"Can't you let me speak normally?" I shouted in Catalan. "It's just a game!" The *normally* came out with so much force, it bounced off the rim of Papa's glasses and fell into his coffee.

"I'm just trying to help you learn, Gala," he said. He straightened his glasses, fished the word out of his cup and switched back to English. "Come on. Let's ~~~~~~ ~~~~~~."

"Maybe ~~~~~~ ~~~~~~, Jordi," Ryan said in a soothing blue, plus some other things that I didn't understand. Ryan didn't like confrontation. He was a bit like Dion, big and tall and almost always in a good mood. Papa and I were more like Celine. We were small and dark-haired, and we both had a bit of a temper. Sometimes I didn't see why he and Ryan liked each other so much. They were completely different.

"She has to practise," Papa said, shaking his head. "It was really difficult for me to learn English at university. It will be easier in the ~~~~~~ if she learns now."

"She will. Just let her ~~~~~~." Ryan swept up the cards and asked me a question in his oddly shaped Catalan. "Would you want to play one more time, Gala?"

I shook my head. The atmosphere had gone sour. "No. I'm going to take the dogs for a walk."

Celine and Dion had been dozing on the sofa, but they both raced to the door when I called them. I wasn't sure where to go, so I let them lead me up the hill and towards the high street. I tried to imagine what I would be doing if I was still in Cadaqués right now. Maybe Papa and I would take a bike ride, or maybe Iaia would come to ours for lunch. Afterwards, I would meet Mariam at the park or go over to Pau's house on my scooter. I'd had Sundays like those just a few weeks ago, but they already felt so far away.

The dogs made a right turn by the bakery, where Celine spotted a seagull and chased it until we arrived at the park.

There were people behind the gate, and as I moved closer I recognized four or five kids from my year group. I didn't know all of their names yet, but one was Craig and one was Abigail – the dark-haired boy and the girl with the long ponytail who sat together in Maths. They were pointing at something near the trees and shouting words I couldn't catch.

When I saw a shock of frizzy blond hair between the branches, my heart leaped. It was Natalie, sitting in the grass. Her head was bent down, and I could tell from the tension in her shoulders that Craig and his friends were bothering her again.

Moving very slowly, I went over to the park gate and pushed it open. The kids didn't notice – Craig was laughing like a hyena now while another girl sang something in a high-pitched voice. I pulled Dion towards me and unclipped the leash from his collar.

"Go, Dion," I whispered, pointing to the kids. "Go! Go!"

I hid behind a bush by the gate as Dion went ambling towards Craig, Abigail and the others. It wasn't exactly the intimidating entrance I was hoping for, but then Celine shot out from between my ankles, yapping and barking loud enough for the whole town to hear. Stirred up by her excitement, Dion picked up the pace and started running towards the kids. To them, this wasn't sixty kilos of cuddles and silliness lumbering towards them. It was a big, snarling Great Dane with jaws that could rip into them like a juicy bit of steak.

"Aaaaaargh!" Craig's scream came out so big, he almost choked on the letters before spinning on his heels and sprinting towards the gate. Abigail and the others followed close behind, dropping trails of 'Go!' and 'Quick!' on to the grass behind them. The last boy slammed the gate shut, which stopped Celine in her tracks. The kids ran down the street, shouting and laughing, and their voices soon faded away. I slipped out from behind the bush and walked towards the trees. Celine was still trying to jump over the gate, but Dion came to join me instead.

"Hello." I felt nervous, and the word came out shaky and pale purple. "I am Gala. He is Dion."

Natalie nodded. There was a pause, then she gave me something like a smile. I lifted my hand and did an awkward wave in return.

"You are OK?" I asked her. "Those…"

I knew lots of not-very-polite words for kids like Craig and Abigail in Spanish and Catalan, but not in English. Natalie nodded again and shrugged, as if to say it wasn't a big deal, even though it was. Dion seemed to think so too because he bounded forward and licked her face. I had been a bit apprehensive around Dion at first, but Natalie just laughed and patted his head.

"Sorry. He is very…" I searched for the right words. I wanted to say that he was loving and protective and cuddly. Instead I said, "Very dog."

Natalie laughed again. It was a light, jingly sound, like a far-off bicycle bell. I sat down in the grass opposite her and started picking out daisies to make a chain. Natalie didn't say anything but her gaze kept flicking towards the grass. I thought she felt uncomfortable with me sitting so close until I realized she was looking for words. Her hand kept twitching by her side, like she wanted to reach out and grab one.

For a moment I wondered if maybe Craig and Abigail and the others made fun of her because of that, but from the way she moved I could tell that she didn't want me to see. They didn't know. It was a secret.

Stroking Dion's ears, I thought about what to do. Natalie might be embarrassed if I told her I'd seen her picking up a word at school on Monday. Then again, I didn't want her to wonder if I thought she was weird, like Eilidh C and the others did.

Eventually I pushed the grass back and looked at the scattered words. Some had been there for a long time – you could tell because their colours were faded – but others were fresh and bright.

Moving slowly, I picked up a word with my thumb and index finger and held it out to Natalie. ***Expected.*** I'd picked it because I liked the neon-yellow shade of the letters, but the feeling I got from it clashed with the colour: it was disappointment, strong and bitter. I almost put it down again but Natalie reached out and took the word from me. She touched its edges with her finger, then looked up at me and smiled. This time it was a proper smile, and it was like switching on the lights on a Christmas tree – it made everything about her sparkle.

"I do not know what is it," I said slowly. "Expected."

She reached into her pocket and gently pulled out a small handful of words. She picked a dark purple one, carefully pulled off the first two letters, then stuck them to the yellow word I'd given her. When she handed it back to me, it read ***unexpected.*** I didn't know what that meant, either, so I took out my phone and opened the app that scanned and translated words into Catalan for me.

"*Inesperat*," the robotic voice read out. Something that might take you by surprise.

We smiled at each other.

There was a loud bark behind me. Celine had finally given up on trying to jump over the gate and was coming to join us. I introduced her to Natalie and went back to searching for more words. The dogs snuffled round the grass, trying to help. Dion proudly presented us with an old chocolate-bar wrapper, and Celine got distracted and started chasing a seagull.

It took Natalie a long time to find words to put in her pocket. I didn't know what sort of thing she liked or was searching for, and I didn't know most of their meanings anyway, so I picked up words that looked interesting or had pretty colours. Dusk in delicate violet. ***Whisk*** in a sleek magenta. **Charm** in bold turquoise. It was odd to feel strangers' emotions when I touched the letters, but it didn't seem like we were doing anything wrong. The words would disappear soon anyway.

Natalie put all the words that I picked into her pocket, so I took that to mean she liked them too. I wanted to know what she'd do with them, how long she'd been collecting words and why. But the whole time we sat together she didn't say anything. Not a single word.

That was OK. I'd had a whole week of listening to a language I could only partly understand. Right now I was happy with silence.

By four o'clock, it was already starting to get dark and very cold. Natalie stood up, brushed the grass from her knees and pointed at the road. I got up too.

"Yes, I will go," I said, following her towards the gate.

I wanted to say that I'd see her on Monday but I couldn't remember how, so I just said goodbye while Celine sniffed her ankles, and Dion jumped up to lick her face. We both laughed, and I was still smiling as I turned on to the road back to Ryan's. I didn't care what those other kids thought of Natalie. I had made a friend.

Seven

The Eilidhs couldn't have lunch with me on Monday because choir practice had started up again. I didn't know the word 'choir' – or why it sounded like it started with a q and not a ch – so Eilidh O explained this by singing and clapping her hands in the middle of the corridor. I laughed and joined in, bobbing my head and waving my hands over my head like I was at a concert.

"You guys, stop!" Eilidh C laughed along but her face had gone bright pink, and she glanced around to see if anyone was watching us before pointing to the music room. "Come with us, Gala! It's 〰〰〰 fun."

I shook my head and said no thank you. I wasn't a good singer, and I probably wouldn't know the songs. The idea of trying to read the lyrics fast enough to be able to join in made my head hurt. What I really wanted to do was go outside and play football or basketball, something that didn't require much talking or listening. But, as usual, it was pouring with rain.

"OK. We'll 〰〰〰 next 〰〰〰 〰〰〰," Eilidh C said.

I thought she was saying that they'd wait for me, and we

could all go to our next class together, but I wasn't sure. I said yes anyway, and they hurried off to the music room to join Olu, Frankie and their other friends. That left me with a problem: now I didn't know who to sit with at lunch.

I thought about going back to Ryan's house. It was only a few minutes' walk from school, and Papa was at home job-hunting, so he'd be there to let me in and make me something to eat. Maybe if he thought I didn't have anyone to have lunch with he'd feel bad about bringing me to Scotland. Maybe, if I pinched the skin between my thumb and index finger really hard or thought about videos I'd seen of lost dogs being reunited with their owners, I could even shed a few tears. It would be another step in my masterplan to make him move home again.

But, as I was heading towards the exit, I saw Natalie in the canteen. She was sitting by herself at a table in the far corner, eating from a lunch box and reading a book. I quickly joined the queue for food and picked a sandwich and a bottle of apple juice from the counter. For my first few days of school I'd brought packed lunches with me too, but the Eilidhs and their friends all bought food with these little plastic lunch cards in the canteen, so I'd asked Papa if I could do the same. I paid for my stuff and hurried over to join her.

"Hello," I said. "I can sit?"

Natalie nodded. She looked surprised, as if this was something unexpected. (I'd memorized that word after she gave it to me on Sunday. I was hoping to use it, but I hadn't had the chance yet.) I sat opposite her, and Natalie put her book down. It was a thick hardback with a drawing of a girl and a lion on the cover.

"It is good?" I asked.

Natalie made a so-so motion with her hand. I took a bite of my sandwich. Sandwiches were more of a morning thing at home, and it seemed strange to eat one for lunch. I'd been in a hurry to join Natalie so I'd just grabbed the first thing I could see. It turned out to be filled with tuna, mayonnaise and sweetcorn. My nose started wrinkling before I'd even finished the first bite.

"This is not good," I said. "This is very, very bad."

Natalie grinned and spun her lunch box towards me. Inside there was a bagel, two cereal bars, a packet of raisins and some fruit. I reached for one of the cereal bars, waited for her to nod OK, then said thank you and unwrapped it. It was a bit dry but better than the horrible fishy thing I'd just paid £1.89 for. Natalie took out a tangerine and peeled it, and we both chewed in silence for a while.

At my old school, there was never any silence between me and my friends at lunchtime: usually we were all shouting over each other to be heard. Mariam always talked with so much force that her words would sometimes land on our faces. One time we let Pau walk around with the word for **pants** stuck to his forehead all afternoon. The idea that we'd ever sit in silence... It was impossible.

But this silence wasn't uncomfortable. Just like at the park, it was a nice break after a whole morning of trying to understand what people were talking about. But a big part of me was still curious about why Natalie wasn't saying anything.

"I can ask... *Can* I ask..." I corrected myself. "You do not talk?"

There was a dark flicker in Natalie's eyes. For a moment

I wished I hadn't brought it up, then she took out her phone and typed something. She put it down in front of me. There was an article called *Selective Mutism* open on the screen. I tried to sound out the title but the words came out of my mouth all jumbled up.

"This is too difficult," I said, shaking my head.

But I hadn't seen that there was a list of language options down the left-hand side of the page. Natalie leaned over and clicked the one for Catalan. My eyebrows shot up. I didn't think anyone here knew that we spoke Catalan *and* Spanish where I came from. Except Ryan, and that was only because he'd been dating my dad for two years.

Natalie gave me half of her bagel, then ate the rest of her lunch while I read the article. It was about an anxiety disorder that made it impossible for people to speak in certain situations or places. They weren't choosing not to speak. The anxiety triggered something called a freeze response that meant that sometimes they physically couldn't do it, even if they really tried.

"School..." I tried to work out how to ask my question. I pointed at the phone. "Is like this for you?"

Natalie nodded. It was the sort of nod that said a lot of things, but I couldn't quite read them all yet.

"And with new people?" Another nod. "But with your family? In your house?"

Natalie smiled. She lifted her hand and opened and closed it like she was playing castanets to show that she talked a lot at home. I smiled.

"My house? In Spain?" I made the same hand movement. "But here?" I mimed zipping my lips.

Natalie grinned. She tapped at her phone, then

passed it back to me. It was now open on the maps app. When I looked up at her, she pointed to me. She wanted me to put an address in. I typed *Cadaqués*. My heart gave a little pang of longing when the map opened on a narrow alleyway with whitewashed walls, deep blue doors and shutters, and balconies half hidden by plants and flowers.

"My city. Look!" I moved the map round the corner and a few streets down and zoomed in. "My friend and me."

Papa had found this when he was showing Ryan directions to somewhere once: an image of Pau and me captured by the mapping company a couple of years ago. We were going down Carrer Curós on our scooters, our left legs bent back at the exact same angle like we were figure skaters. Looking at it now, I could feel the way the scooter wobbled over the cobblestones. The warmth of the sun on the back of my neck and the tickling of the bougainvillea against my bare arm when we brushed past it. I liked the idea that some part of us was still there, zipping down that street in the sun.

Natalie's eyes had lit up. She grabbed the phone and tapped at the screen again. When she turned it round, the map was open on an image of a library in Inverness. Papa had taken me there last weekend to borrow some books in English, but I hadn't opened them yet. Natalie swiped to move the image to the right until a small figure with lots of frizzy blond hair came into the frame. She was crossing the road, holding a huge stack of books.

"You too!" I said, laughing.

It was a funny coincidence, both of us having map versions of ourselves to show one another. Maybe they'd meet in the digital dimension and become friends too.

We sat together until the bell rang, looking up our favourite places. Natalie showed me a place called the Fairy Glen and a second-hand bookshop that she loved. I picked the cove where Papa and I used to go snorkelling and the village that Iaia came from in Mallorca. Then I moved on to pictures of Celine and Dion, just like I'd done with Eilidh O. Natalie didn't have any pets but she showed me photos of her little sister, Ava, who was one and a half and super cute. Natalie didn't speak, and I couldn't say even half the things I was thinking, but little by little I was able to put together a picture of her life. When the bell rang to tell us to go back to class, I pointed at the table.

"Tomorrow?" I asked Natalie. "Here again?"

She smiled and nodded. As we got up to leave, I noticed my words were scattered across the canteen table. It was less than I'd produce in five minutes back home, but the most I'd spoken since coming here. And, for the first time, it had almost felt natural.

Eight

After that, I spent every lunchtime with Natalie. I was worried the Eilidhs would be hurt that I wasn't sitting with them any more, so the second time I asked them to join us too. Eilidh O said OK but Eilidh C didn't look so keen. She started whispering to Eilidh O, salmon-pink words that came out too fast for me to follow. In the end, they said they'd sit with Frankie, Olu and the others as usual and left me and Natalie by ourselves.

"Just ~~~~~~ if you want to sit with us again, Gala," Eilidh C said, her smile fading slightly as she looked towards the table where Natalie was half hidden behind another big book.

It wasn't that I didn't like the Eilidhs. I really did. Eilidh C reminded me of my friend Pau back home – she talked constantly, and she had a quick comeback for everything. Eilidh O had the most infectious laugh ever, and she helped me out a lot when I didn't understand things in class.

But, for some reason, I found I could talk in English much more around Natalie than I could with them or anyone else in my class, or even Papa and Ryan. There were no expectations with Natalie. She didn't correct my mistakes, like Papa. She didn't act as if it was a big deal whenever I said a full sentence, like the Eilidhs. She also didn't need or want me to talk, like it seemed everyone else did. If we sat in silence for ages, that was fine. There were other ways for us to communicate – we started messaging each other loads after school, and we wrote notes on our phones or in our textbooks when we had something important to say.

One Friday lunchtime, while we were both drawing in the back of our school planners in the library, Natalie sent me a paper plane she'd made from a page ripped out of her English jotter. There was a message written on the wing:

Do you want to come to my house after school?

I wrote my reply on the nose:

Yes! with a drawing of a smiling cat beside it, even though I'm definitely a dog person. Cats are just easier to draw.

Before my last class, I sent Papa a message to tell him that I'd be home late because I was going to a friend's house. We had PE last – Natalie was in Ryan's class but I was with Ms O'Connor – so I waited for her outside the changing rooms after the bell rang. Ryan came out of the gym, carrying some tattered blue gymnastics mats.

"Hey, Gala!" His eyes lit up. "Are you ~~~~~~ netball?"

Ryan had been asking me to join the school netball team since we arrived in Fortrose. I'd never even heard of netball before moving here – he said it was like basketball, but with no dribbling or running with the ball. I was tempted to try it, but I kept saying no. If I joined a team, Papa would think I'd accepted that we were here for the long haul, and I definitely hadn't.

"No, no netball." My words were pale grey, their usual colour when I spoke to Ryan these days. "I go with Natalie to her house."

Ryan looked disappointed but he smiled. "Oh, that's great. You'll be back for tea?"

I knew by now that when Ryan said 'tea' he meant dinner, not the drink. That had confused me when we first arrived – I kept wondering why he wasn't pouring himself cups of Yorkshire Gold with his stir-fry or fajitas.

"OK. At seven thirty, yes?"

Ryan grinned. Back in Cadaqués, Papa and I always ate dinner at around nine o'clock but Ryan got hungry really quickly and had tried to talk us down to six. That seemed ridiculously early to us, so he and Papa had come to a compromise of 7.30 p.m. "Yup. See you then."

Natalie came out of the changing rooms, so I said goodbye to Ryan and grabbed the sleeve of her jacket to hurry her away. We stopped by the shop on the high street to buy some sweets and crisps, then walked up the hill to her house. It was a small white cottage with a slide and swing set in the front garden, only five minutes away from Ryan's. When we reached the door, Natalie turned to me and smiled.

"Here it is," she said, stepping into the warmth. "Our humble ~~~~~~."

It was the first time I'd ever heard her speak. Even though she'd told me she talked lots at home, it caught me off guard and I missed the last word. I tried not to show that I was surprised. Sometimes at school I'd go for ages without talking too, and I didn't like it when people made a big fuss when I finally said something. But it was nice to hear her voice. It was soft and lower than I'd expected, and her words were formed from ***cute, chunky letters*** that flicked out at the tips. Right now they were a welcoming dark red, like a cosy Christmas jumper.

She kicked off her shoes in the hallway, so I did the same before following her inside. The kitchen was a small, warm room with sunflower-yellow walls, a round wooden table and a black Aga like the one Ryan had at his house. Natalie's little sister Ava was in her high chair, swinging her legs and eating a biscuit while their mum cut up some cucumber sticks.

"Hi, love. This must be the ~~~~~~ Gala." Natalie's mum had frizzy blond hair just like her daughter's. Her words were a similar shape to Natalie's too, round and chunky. "I'm Abby. Really nice to ~~~~~~ meet you."

I said it was nice to meet her too. Abby asked Natalie how school had been. There was a worried blue hue to her words. Natalie told her it was fine and slumped into the seat beside Ava, who was even cuter in person: she had big brown eyes and sticky-out ears, and she was wearing a jumper with a sequinned elephant on it.

"Can you say hi to Gala, Avie?" Natalie asked. Her words turned the same warm yellow as the walls.

Ava waved her biscuit at me. There were crumbs and letters all round her mouth and down her clothes. "That!" she said, and then a whole load of sounds that came out looking like musical notes in pastel colours: **ba**, **la**, **da**, **ma**, **pa**... Natalie kissed the top of her head, then carefully picked up the **that** and put it in her pocket.

"Let's go to my room."

Abby insisted we have something healthy to eat before

we tucked into the sweets and crisps in our hands, so we went upstairs carrying half of Ava's cucumber sticks and an apple each. When Natalie pushed open the door to her room, I gasped. There was a world map on her wall, a huge doughnut pillow on her bed, and books *everywhere*. Books crammed into the shelves and piled on top of the desk, stacks on the floor like towers and scattered over the bed. It would have taken me a thousand years to read that many.

"Wow! Books like you very much," I said, then realized that didn't sound right. "No, *you* like books very much."

Natalie laughed and put the snacks down on her desk. "I hope books like me too."

She gestured to the pile and told me to borrow as many as I liked. I shook my head – reading in English was still hard, and I didn't want to do any more of it than was strictly necessary – but I did want to look at the covers. As I gazed at the spines of the stack on her bedside table, I noticed a small wooden box on her desk. It was decorated with carvings of tortoises and filled with words, some bright and new, some very faded.

"One question," I said. "What you do with these?"

Natalie took today's word collection from the pocket of her school trousers and dropped them into the box. "I save them."

"Save them?"

"I call it wordsearching." She reached under the bed and pulled out a large, square photo album like the ones Iaia had at her house. "This is for Ava. It's a ~~~~~ of her first words. Like those Baby's First Words books, but ~~~~~ for her."

Inside the album weren't pictures, but words: ***mama***, ***dada, bye-bye, bus,*** all in a toddler's large, wobbly letters.

As I flicked through the pages, Natalie took a pink silk cloth from her desk drawer. Moving slowly, she pressed Ava's ***that*** to a page. The letters curled up round the edges so Natalie patted them very gently with the silk cloth.

"This way they don't disappear," she said as she folded the cloth neatly into a square.

"I do not know…" I started to say, then trailed off because I wasn't sure how to phrase what I wanted to say. I had seen saved speech before – we once went on a school trip to a museum in Barcelona that had framed spoken words taken from speeches by famous politicians and artists. But I didn't know you could do it like this.

With the help of a translation app on her phone, Natalie explained that she'd started playing around with placing spoken words on paper last year, trying to find a way to stop them from disintegrating, until she'd found the right method. She told me that some cultures always save babies' first words – that was where she'd got the idea for Ava's book – and that others hold on to dying people's final sentences, passing them down through generations.

It made me wonder why it wasn't more common. At Ryan's house, we swept our words off the table and other surfaces or hoovered them up from the floor, same as most people. I'd never thought about doing anything with them. Thinking about it now, it seemed strange that no one else had ever suggested it.

"It's best to put them on paper a few hours after they've been ~~~~~~, when they're still fresh. I make ~~~~~~

with them too," Natalie said.

Seeing I hadn't caught the word, she picked it up from the carpet and showed it to me. ***Poems***. It was a soft, shy lavender and smaller than the words she'd spoken until now. "Poetry. Like this."

She went to her bed and pulled a notebook out from under her pillow. On the first page was a haiku, a Japanese form of poetry made from five, seven then five syllables. I knew about those because Papa had bought English poetry magnets to put on Ryan's fridge, and he was always making haikus with them.

Lonely **volcano**,

Thinking, bubbling, *hissing*, **hot**.

Come on, *do* **it**. **Blow!**

Each of the words had been spoken by a different person – I could tell from the sizes, colours and fonts.

"You do this with the words? Make poems?"

Natalie nodded. Her cheeks had gone a little pink. "Yes. Sometimes. I know I could just write them, or make them with my own speech. But I prefer to use other people's words."

"Why?"

"Speaking seems so *easy* for most people. They just talk and talk. The words come out, and they don't think anything of it, but it's so hard for me."

She picked up a light yellow ***star*** from the box and turned it in her fingers.

"This way it feels like ... like I can take some of that simpleness and have it for myself, you know? That those words that come so easily can be mine too. I don't always have to fight for them."

I read the haiku again. I didn't know the words bubbling, *hissing* or **blow**, but even so the poem felt sad and a little angry. "What does it want to say?"

Natalie turned the book round to look at the words. "It's about how I feel sometimes, when I want to speak but can't. The words are there but they get stuck at the back of my throat. I can feel them building up inside me, and the pressure gets higher and higher until I feel like I'm about to explode."

She talked very slowly so I could read each word, but I still wasn't sure what she meant. She coughed then made an exploding gesture with her hand to show me:

words flying everywhere, a whole day's

worth of thoughts she hadn't been able to say.

I nodded quickly. That was exactly the way I felt after a long week of school too.

"That's what some people don't understand. It's not that I don't *want* to talk," she said. "Well, actually, sometimes I don't – sometimes I don't have anything to say, or I'd rather just listen. Some people aren't worth replying to."

I didn't know the word *worth*, but I could guess just what she meant. "Like Craig and Abigail?"

Natalie nodded. "Them, and others. Sometimes I think

the world would be a better place if people didn't talk so much. But a lot of the time I really do want to say something, and I can't. My body won't let me. It's ~~~~~~."

The word caught in a fold of her school jumper: *frustrating*. "It is like this for me too," I said. "People think I cannot speak very well, so maybe I am not smart."

"That annoys me." A red tinge seeped into Natalie's fern-green words. "Most of them don't know a word of your language, or any other language! You know two, *and* lots of English."

"So, what you want to say is … I am a genius?" I said, making my tone serious and the words briefcase brown.

Natalie laughed and said, "Exactly!"

I grinned, happy that she'd understood that I was joking and that I'd made her laugh. It was the longest conversation we'd had, maybe the longest conversation I'd ever had in English. But I didn't leave Natalie's house an hour later feeling tired and like I wanted to go home, the way I'd left school every single day. I went away feeling like we were both finally being heard.

Nine

That Saturday, I woke up to the smell of something sweet baking downstairs. Clinking cups and plates and a murmur of voices told me that Papa and Ryan were already awake. They always got up early at the weekends – Ryan went for a jog as soon as the sun rose, and Papa liked to have a cup of coffee and read the news online first thing – but that baking smell was unusual. I got up, put on a jumper and my koala slippers and went downstairs. When I walked into the kitchen, Ryan spun round to greet me wearing oven gloves and holding a baking tray.

"Ensaïmades!" he announced. "Well, my ~~~~~~ at ensaïmades."

An ensaïmada was a type of pastry from Mallorca, where my Iaia came from. When Ryan used to visit us back home, we always bought them from the bakery two blocks along from our flat. They were shaped in a spiral with powdered sugar on top and were one of my favourite things to eat. There were six on the tray plus another six on a cooling rack.

"Thank you," I said. The words came out bright yellow, the way they always did when I was really happy about something. “They are very beautiful.”

Ryan was saying something about not being able to find one of the ingredients. Papa squeezed his shoulder and said they looked delicious, even though he doesn’t actually like ensaïmades or anything too sugary. He poured another cup of coffee and made himself some toast while we waited for the pastries to cool.

“What do you want to do today, Gala?” Papa asked me in English.

Iaia and I had promised we would always video call after she played padel with her friends on Saturday mornings, and I couldn’t miss that. But the sky was blue for the first time since we’d arrived in Scotland, so I didn’t want to spend all day inside, either.

“Maybe walk?” I asked Papa in English as I sat down at the kitchen table. “With Celine and Dion.”

Dion had been dozing in his bed in the corner but he looked up and made a curious *mmph?* sound when he heard his name. Celine was in the back garden, yapping furiously at a squirrel who had dared to set foot in her territory.

Papa smiled. “Of course. We can go anywhere you like.”

Ryan was holding a bag of powdered sugar and a sieve over the tray of cooling ensaïmades. He asked me how much to put on, and I kept gesturing for more and more until Papa laughed and said you weren’t supposed to have more sugar than pastry. Then Ryan set two ensaïmades on the table and sat down beside me.

“*Bon profit!*” he said. That meant ‘enjoy your meal’ in Catalan, and Ryan always said it before we ate. The words came out looking a little strange, with the o too bold and the i too slim, but it always made Papa do this goofy smile.

We picked up our pastries at exactly the same time and both took a big bite.

As soon as I started to chew, I knew it was all wrong. This didn't taste like an ensaïmada at all. It was far too dry, almost like a bagel, and despite all the sugar the pastry wasn't sweet enough. It wasn't bad but it definitely wasn't an ensaïmada. It wasn't even close.

"Hmm, needs a bit of ~~~~~~," Ryan said, pulling a face. "Sorry, Gala. I'll try again."

I wanted to say it was OK but my words had clogged up suddenly. It wasn't the same, and I had really wanted it to be. It's not that I wasn't grateful – it was just that, for a moment, I'd thought I was going to get a little taste of home. To my horror, I realized my eyes were watering. I put down the not-an-ensaïmada and rubbed them quickly.

"Gala! What's the matter with you?" Papa asked me in Catalan. His words scattered across the table, all deep amber tones and sharp edges. "Why are you crying?"

"Is it that bad?" Ryan forced a laugh but I could tell from the navy shade of his words that he was disappointed. "I'm really sorry, Gala. I was just…"

I tried to say that wasn't it at all, but the tears were starting to fall, and I couldn't speak. I turned round and ran upstairs to my bedroom. A draught slammed the door shut behind me with a loud bang. I leaped on to my bed and hid my face in the pillow until the fabric was wet with my tears. After a moment, quick, heavy footsteps followed me up the stairs. Papa opened the door without knocking and came inside.

"What's got into you?" he asked. "Ryan went to a lot of

effort to make those for you, Gala. You could at least have said thank you."

"I did say thank you," I said, my words pressing into the pillow. "It was nice of him to make the ensaïmades."

"Then why are you acting like this? This isn't like you."

I lifted my head to look him in the eye. "Because I want to go home. I want to go back to Cadaqués!"

Papa sat down on the bed as I squashed my face back into the pillow. He let out a long sigh. "We're going there at Easter. The time will pass so quickly, you'll see."

I hated the thought of going to Cadaqués as a visitor. Everyone there used to complain about tourists in the summer, how bad the traffic became and how busy the beaches were. Papa would moan about them loads too, even though he and Ryan met when Ryan was on holiday with his friends in Barcelona. Going for a holiday would feel like being a tourist in my own town. Those streets were my streets. I didn't want to have to say goodbye to them all over again.

"It's normal to be homesick," Papa said. "I miss my friends too, my co-workers, my running group. But they're still there! It just means we'll really appreciate the time we have with them when we go back."

"Why can't I go and live with Iaia?" I asked, ignoring him. "She has a spare room. I bet she'd say yes."

"Because I'd miss you too much, Galeta. Wouldn't you miss me?"

I didn't answer, though of course the answer was yes.

Papa rubbed my back. "I'm sorry, bug. It wasn't an easy decision. But I really think it's what was best for our family. All three of us."

I didn't know how he could think it was best for me. I was crying properly now and couldn't reply. Papa started to stroke my hair but I jerked my head to the left, and he took his hand away. Soon I ran out of sobs and everything was silent except for the seagulls cawing and the waves whispering as they rushed towards the beach. It was too quiet, this place. It made me quiet too. I wasn't supposed to be like that. I was supposed to be big yellow words under a bright blue sky.

"You know, you still haven't decorated your room much," Papa said, looking round at the empty walls. "How about we go into town after our walk and buy some new posters? Or we could get some photos of you and your friends printed and put them up."

Before we moved here, Ryan had painted the walls of this room my favourite colour, raspberry pink, and Papa ordered me a new desk, bookshelves, and a galaxy lamp that made the walls sparkle with millions of blue and purple stars. I had to admit it was quite nice. But they couldn't bring me the little green parrots that landed on my balcony back home or the chattering from the café on the street below. Pau and Mariam and Laia would never be in this room; we would never scream with laughter and tell each other secrets like we had before.

"This isn't my room," I snapped. "It's never going to be my room."

Papa gave another long, frustrated sigh. "It is, Gala. This is home. We live here now." His words were midnight blue, and they fell to the carpet like raindrops.

He stood up and went to the door without looking back. "You need to get used to it."

We live here now

Ten

I had another big cry after my fight with Papa. My eyes were still red when I spoke to Iaia, and then she got all worried and sad, and that made me cry even more. Afterwards, Papa came upstairs to give me a hug and said he was sorry he got mad, and then Ryan brought the dogs up to see me. He apologized too and said some stuff I couldn't follow, while Dion tried to climb on to my lap, and Celine fought with my stuffed shark. I told Ryan in Catalan that it wasn't his fault and that actually I thought it was nice that he'd tried to make something from home for me. He looked a bit confused but I think he got the gist of it because he gave me a big hug too. He smelled like his not-ensaïmades.

Papa insisted that we still go for our walk and then into Inverness to buy some things for my room, but a stiff atmosphere lingered round the house for the rest of the weekend. I was actually looking forward to going back to school on Monday, especially to lunchtime with Natalie. She listened while I told her about the argument and how much I missed home.

"We go back in … um, *abril*? April! But that is very…" I searched for the word for far away, but couldn't find it.

"Sad," I said instead.

We were between two stacks of bookshelves in the library. Natalie had told me she often found interesting words here, maybe from the librarians recommending certain books or kids talking about stories they had read. The place was busy, as it always was at lunchtime – people came to use the computers, play games or do last-minute homework for their next classes. I stood with my back to the room so no one could see Natalie pick through the words scattered on the floor.

"There are good things here," I continued. "You. Celine and Dion. The Eilidhs. But my friends…"

I'd forgotten how to say that I missed them, but Natalie looked at me and nodded to show she understood what I meant. She took a book with a picture of a pirate on the cover from the shelf and opened it. Dozens of words fell on to the floor. Her eyes lit up, and she leaned forward to look through them.

I glanced over my shoulder: Craig and Abigail and some of their group were crowded round one of the library computers, watching as Luke Watkins played a shooting game. I was worried they'd spot Natalie and say something nasty to her again, but they didn't look our way.

"Maybe I say I am very, very sad, and my father will go home," I said, though I was starting to wonder if that was true. We'd been in Scotland for four weeks now. That was a whole month of telling Papa how homesick I was, and a whole month of him insisting I would learn to love it here. But, even so, I'd keep trying. He would have to take me seriously eventually.

Natalie didn't look up from the words on the floor.

I felt a little pang of guilt. If we went back to Cadaqués now, I would miss her just like I missed Pau and Mariam and Laia.

"You can visit!" I said. "I think you like it there."

She smiled then opened her schoolbag and took out one of her jotters. There was a cheer from the computers then – Luke had completed the game. Ms Walsh the librarian came over to tell them to be quiet, but Craig was shouting and pushing another boy out of the way for his turn.

Out of everyone in our year, Craig and Abigail were the only people who I really didn't like. They said mean things to Natalie in every single Maths class, and sometimes in the corridors too. They always spoke too fast for me to hear exactly what they said, but I would glower at them from across the room, and sometimes they noticed. Going back home would mean leaving Natalie alone with them again.

When I turned round, Natalie was placing the words from the pirate book on a piece of paper ripped from her jotter. She took a silk cloth just like the one she had at home from her bag, patted them gently, then handed the page to me. It was another short poem.

Home is a treasure *that* **can** never *be buried*,

A *ship* that can never **be** sunk.

Pieces *of* gold, parts *of* the ***past.***

Away with maps – ***there's*** a compass *in* your ***heart.***

"This is for me?" I said, blinking at Natalie. "This is very nice!"

She shrugged modestly. I read the poem again. I couldn't believe Natalie had put it together so quickly. I knew all the words except *buried*, sunk and compass, but I could guess what they meant, so that made me happy. But more than that I felt something from the poem. Like, no matter how long or far away I was from Cadaqués, it would still be waiting for me.

"Thank you," I said. Then I remembered a phrase Ryan said a lot and added, "Thanks a million."

Natalie grinned, and the bell rang for the next class.

I kept the poem hidden in my bag until the end of school so no one else would see it. As soon as I got back to my bedroom that afternoon, I took it out to read again. Natalie could have written the same thing with a pen, but there was something different about using people's speech. It was as if all the thoughts and emotions that had gone into those words had seeped into the poem, infusing it with feelings. The fact that she'd rescued words that would otherwise disappear and made something new with them, just for me … it was special.

The photos that Papa had printed to decorate my room when we went into Inverness on Saturday were still in a yellow envelope on my desk. He'd also bought me some Blu-tack to put them up, so I added four dots to the back of the paper that Natalie had set the poem on and hung it beside my window. When I was looking at the blank grey sea and the cloudy sky, I would read it and remember that home was still out there, somewhere beyond the horizon.

"Gala!" Papa called up from the bottom of the stairs. "Don't you want a snack?"

"Yes! I'm getting dressed!"

I pulled off my uniform and got changed into my own clothes. On my way out of my room, I saw a word shimmering on the carpet. Right now Papa filled a lot of his day with cleaning, so by the time I got home from school there weren't many words lying around the house. This one was one of Ryan's. It was a shiny pale purple whisper and made of his usual simple, rounded letters: *faith*.

Crouching down, I picked the word up and slid it on to my palm. The letters caught the glow from the big light above me and lit up in sparkling indigo. I wasn't sure what it meant, but the colour was pretty, and it left me with a warm, safe feeling. As if everything was going to be OK.

Going back to my room, I looked around for something to put the word in and found an old French biscuit tin that Iaia had given me a few years ago. I'd always used it for pens and random bits and pieces, but now I emptied everything into the top drawer of my desk and placed the word inside, moving slowly like I'd seen Natalie do so that it didn't break. When I looked up the definition of *faith* on my phone, I smiled. It was the perfect word to kick off my very own collection.

Eleven

There was a bad case of flu going round the school – Natalie and I were both off with it the next week, and then it was Eilidh C's turn. Our classes felt much quieter without her constantly chattering and cracking jokes, but I had to admit it was easier to talk to Eilidh O when it was just the two of us. We sat together in all our classes and spent most of the time giggling. Every day, we found another thing we had in common: we both loved salted-caramel ice cream, we both hated olives, and we both really wanted to go to Australia, mostly to see koalas.

Eilidh O loved languages too (as well as English, she spoke Igbo, her dad's first language, and her favourite subjects were French and German) so she always wanted to know how to say things in Catalan and Spanish. When Eilidh C was there too, she'd get bored and change the subject, but now Eilidh O could ask me as many questions as she liked. There was still so much I didn't know about English. It made me feel good to be the one giving the answers.

But on Thursday something changed. When I got to registration, Eilidh O was quiet and seemed sad. She let me borrow one of her cute pens in Science, like she always did, but she didn't ask what the Spanish word for the parrots drawn all over it was. She just kept her head down and doodled stars on the edge of her workbook as Mrs Brunner talked to us about DNA.

"Are you OK?" I whispered when Mrs Brunner paused to draw a double helix on the whiteboard.

Eilidh O looked up. "Not really. I ~~~~~~ some bad news yesterday."

Her voice trailed off, and her words became too small and pale for me to read properly. I waited until she was ready, and then she cleared her throat and explained again. She had found out the day before that she'd need an operation later in the year. It wasn't a serious problem but she would have to be put to sleep with a general anaesthetic.

"I'm scared," Eilidh said, her words thin and greyish blue. "What if I don't wake up?"

"You will wake," I said confidently. "The doctors… They make many operations every day."

"You're probably right. But what if mine is the one that goes wrong?"

Mrs Brunner told us to stop talking then, so we got on with our work. I sneakily drew an alpaca in medical scrubs giving a thumbs up and saying, "Everything will be OK!" to make Eilidh smile. She'd cheered up a bit by English and, by the time we went to double PE after break, she was back to her usual chatty self.

Even so, I felt bad that I hadn't been able to say more to make her feel better about the operation. At lunchtime, she headed to extra choir practice for a competition that was coming up, and I went to find Natalie.

"I want to make a poem," I told her as soon as I sat down at our usual table in the canteen. "It is for Eilidh Obiaka."

I told her about Eilidh's operation and how worried she was. Natalie nodded sympathetically, but she looked nervous. Natalie's word collection (and my small one, now with around twenty-five words in the tin in my bedroom) was a secret – it was *our* secret. But I had an idea. I would leave the letter in Eilidh's bag when she wasn't looking, so she wouldn't know it had come from me. I wasn't sure how many other people she'd told about the operation, so we wouldn't mention it directly. It would just be something to make her feel good, like Natalie's poem had done for me.

It was hard to explain all of this but I did the best I could, then pushed my words on to the canteen floor so no one would spot them. Natalie chewed on a cereal bar for a long moment, thinking, then tucked the empty wrapper back in her lunch box and pointed to the door. I followed her out into the courtyard, where a bunch of second years were playing volleyball without a net, and round the back of the gym. This was where the teachers parked their cars (except Ryan, since we lived close enough to walk) and where the school's recycling bins were kept.

Natalie slipped in between two cars and sat on the edge of the wall. "There's never anyone here at lunchtime," she said quietly. "I used to come here to look for words. The cleaners never ~~~~~~ the ones between the cars."

It was the first time she'd talked to me at school. It was probably because there was nobody else here, but it made me feel happy that Natalie was comfortable enough around me to do so. I squeezed on to the wall beside her and watched as she pulled out a handful of words.

After double-checking there was no one watching us, I reached into my pocket.

"I have these." I took out the three words that I'd collected this morning: a *twisting* that I'd found on the floor in Biology; *hopefully*, said by Eilidh O in delicate purple letters; and a cornflower-blue *breath* that got stuck to my sleeve while I was paying for my baked potato in the canteen. I didn't know what any of them meant but I took them because I liked the way they looked.

When I first told Natalie that I'd started wordsearching, I was worried she might be annoyed. It was her thing after all, and she'd been doing it for much longer than me. Instead her face lit up, and she said she'd show me the best ways to fix words to different surfaces. She even brought me a square of pink silk cloth just like the one she used to pat them down on paper, but I hadn't tried it out yet. I wanted to wait until I knew just what to do with the words I'd collected.

Sitting behind the gym, we pooled all our words together and looked through them. Natalie lined them up neatly on her leg. "First things first. What do you want the poem to say?"

"That Eilidh is... I do not know the word," I said. "In Catalan it is *valent.*"

"*Valent...*" Natalie echoed, looking at the word that had fallen to the ground. "Oh, like *valiant*! Do you mean brave?'

"Brave! Yes!" I did know that one after all – Papa had made me watch a film with that title to practise my English before we moved here. "We can make a poem about to be brave."

Natalie reached down and picked up some of the words that had just fallen from our mouths. I took out my English jotter and found a new page for her to place them on. Watching her make the poem was quite amazing. Her hands moved so quickly I couldn't keep track, and her eyes shone in a way I hadn't seen before. She spoke a few more words into her hand to fill in the blanks, then moved the page round for me to see.

Brave is *a first* step.

Brave is to *say* **yes**.

Brave is a ***deep*** *breath*.

Brave *is*

"I don't know what the last line should be," Natalie said, rubbing her chin. "Do you have any ideas?"

I looked down at my feet. There was a small green you just beside the wheel of one of the cars. I picked it up, slid it into place and looked at Natalie. After a moment, she smiled and dabbed it with the cloth.

"Perfect."

We had Design and Technology after lunch, so I slipped the poem into Eilidh O's bag while she went to the machines to sand the wooden box she was making. I was all nervous and jittery for the rest of the lesson, waiting for her to notice the piece of paper, but Eilidh didn't even glance at her bag until we got to our next class. Finally she reached inside for her pencil case, found the page and unfolded it. She was quiet for a moment, reading the words.

"Do you know what this is?" she whispered to me.

I looked at the poem and frowned, pretending I was having trouble understanding the words. "What it says?"

Eilidh O looked at me for a moment, like she was trying to work something out, but then she turned back to the page. "Someone must have 〰〰〰 it into my bag. Did you see anyone?"

My heart was thumping but I shook my head and tried to keep my expression blank. Eilidh O looked round the room. For a moment I was worried that she didn't like the poem, but when she turned round there was a small smile on her face.

"Maybe it was Olu or Amina. I told them about my operation at lunchtime." She moved the paper closer to her face. "It's written with 〰〰〰, though! Other people's words! Have you seen anything like this before?"

I shook my head again and asked her what *brave* meant, just to really throw her off the scent. Eilidh explained, then read the poem again, her lips moving silently as she mouthed the words. The smile on her face was growing wider.

"They're right whoever they are. The operation's probably not so 〰〰〰. I just need to be brave." She looked at me. "It's going to be fine, isn't it?"

"Yes," I said, the word a warm ochre. "Yes, it will be fine."

As Eilidh tucked the poem gently back into her bag, I turned away to hide my grin. Maybe it was only for a few minutes but Natalie and I had used words to make a friend feel better. That was something special, even if they hadn't come directly from us. Maybe especially because they hadn't come from us. We had taken the words that were hard for us to say and claimed them for ourselves.

Eilidh's **brave** was lying on the desk, the colour of honey. I quickly picked it up and put it in my pocket. Most days, English felt like a huge continent that I could never fully travel across. But, every time I added a word to my collection, I took a step forward.

Twelve

Even though I kept wordsearching, I didn't plan on asking Natalie to make any more poems. It had come to me as a way to cheer Eilidh O up, nothing more than that. But a week later Natalie suggested we create one for someone else. This time it was for Frankie McAllister.

Frankie was good friends with the Eilidhs and was in Class 1B with Natalie. That morning, they had told some kids in Geography that they were non-binary and would like people to use the pronouns 'they' and 'them' when talking about them. Most people smiled and said OK or asked a few questions and went back to learning about cloud formations, but others made some nasty comments behind their back. Those words had floated over to Frankie and, from what Natalie had heard, they were really upset.

"What words?" I asked, but I could tell from the way her nose wrinkled that Natalie didn't want to repeat them.

"Oh, you know. Just the usual *hilarious* jokes," she said, the letters sloping with her sarcasm.

We were sitting on the wall around the back of the PE department again. It had become our go-to spot when it wasn't raining. Sometimes we looked through the words that Natalie had found that day, or sometimes we just played games on my phone or doodled in our books. Some days Natalie didn't talk much or at all but on others, like today, she was quite chatty.

"I feel 〰〰〰 bad," Natalie said, reaching into the bag of crisps that we were sharing. "I wanted to tell them to shut up, but 〰〰〰 I couldn't."

She was talking a little too fast for me to catch everything she said but I could tell from the tightness in her voice and the reddish-brown colour of the words that she felt angry and frustrated.

"I know how it feels to be different, and to be called names. I wish I could have 〰〰〰 for them." Natalie picked up a silvery **wonder** off the floor and held it up to the light. "I thought a poem could be a way of saying… I don't know. That we 〰〰〰 Frankie. That it's good to be yourself instead of trying to 〰〰〰 into the boxes other people create for us. Maybe it's a silly idea."

"No, I think it is nice! But now these are two poems we write. What if –" I popped a crisp into my mouth and chewed, trying to find the right words – "somebody learn our secret?"

"They won't if we're careful. Besides, I don't think anyone will think it's us. No one even sees me here. Except Craig and Abigail, and they'd probably assume I couldn't do something like that. They think there's nothing in my head."

There were lots of things I wanted to say to that. Mainly that Natalie's head must be a pretty amazing place, full of colour and stories. Instead I made circles with my thumbs and forefingers and held them to my eyes like glasses.

"I see you."

Natalie laughed and put two curled fists to her eye, pretending to look through a telescope. "I see you too."

"What did you see before we are friends?" I flipped my hair over my shoulder. "You think I am amazing and incredible and astounding, right?"

"Oh yeah. The most astounding."

We both laughed. We'd found that word trapped between the ring pull from a can in the courtyard the day before, and for some reason it had stuck with me, so I kept using it.

"Honestly, I thought you looked a bit … lost. Not just because of the language. Physically lost, like you were somewhere you weren't meant to be."

"That is how I feel. Lost. With no map or one of those…" I cupped one hand into a circle and made a spinning finger with the other. "A *brúixola*."

"A compass," Natalie said, passing me the word to keep. "Do you still feel like that?"

I wasn't sure how to answer. I still wanted to go home, of course. But in the past few weeks I'd found more things that I liked about Fortrose. The way the fields sparkled on frosty mornings. The quiet when Papa and I went on long walks through the woods behind the village, the only sounds our footsteps and birds twittering around us. The strawberry tarts from the bakery on the high street and warming my feet up on the Aga in the kitchen after I'd been outside, especially if Ryan made me a hot chocolate at the same time. This place wasn't home, but it wasn't the strange grey planet I'd landed on at the beginning of January, either.

Instead of replying, I took the notebook from Natalie's hands and opened to a new page. "Come on. Now we make a poem for Frankie."

The next day, we both got to school extra early and slipped the poem through the door of Frankie's locker. Most people didn't use their lockers that much but Frankie played the clarinet and I had seen them put it in there so they didn't have to lug it around all day before orchestra practice. Part of me wanted to hang about and watch them find the poem, but it would look suspicious if Natalie and I were lurking in the corridor for too long.

Gossip travelled fast in our year but no one brought up the poem all morning. I'd almost given up hope when Natalie and I spotted Frankie join the canteen queue with Olu, Scott and the Eilidhs at lunchtime. Frankie was smiling and showing something to Eilidh O. When they turned the corner, my stomach flipped. They were looking at a small piece of lined paper.

"*Mira!*" I whispered to Natalie, the word 'look' accidentally coming out in Catalan because I was so excited. "They have the poem."

The group paid for their food and took the table behind ours. Frankie placed the paper carefully beside their tray. Eilidh O sat down next to them, then spun round and tapped me on the shoulder.

"Remember that poem I found in my bag? Frankie got one too!"

"Really?" I made my eyes wide. "What it says?"

Frankie heard my question and passed me the poem.

I put it in the middle of the table, and Natalie leaned towards it, both of us pretending to read for the first time the words that we'd put together just yesterday.

"It is nice," I said, glancing at Natalie.

She nodded and quickly looked back down at her lunch box, faking a sudden interest in the falafel wrap that her parents had packed for her today.

Olu asked Frankie who had sent the poem, but they said they had no idea. Their eyes narrowed as they studied everyone around the table in turn. "It definitely wasn't any of you?"

Everyone shook their head, including me. Scott said he thought it could be Amina, but Olu said something about how that wasn't possible – Amina was off today and, besides, she wasn't good at keeping secrets. Eilidh O thought it might be Leonie MacDonald, since she loved English and was always writing fanfic, but the others didn't seem to think that was likely.

"What about you, Natalie?" Eilidh C asked. "Do you know who it could be?"

Natalie's cheeks turned pink but she shook her head. Eilidh C smiled and shrugged, and eventually they all turned back round to eat their lunch. I caught Natalie's eye, and we both let out a long, slow sigh of relief.

It made sense that no one thought it was me – I still couldn't speak around the Eilidhs and their friends the way I could with Natalie, and the poem had some complicated words like **gem** and **spectrum** that I hadn't known before Natalie found them yesterday. Nobody would think I could have made that poem by myself because I couldn't. Not yet.

But it was strange that no one had guessed it might be Natalie. I'd seen her slip words into her pocket in the canteen, in Maths class, while we were walking down the corridor, and I'd been here less than two months. Everyone else had started school together back in August, and some kids had even been at primary school with Natalie. She told me she began wordsearching when she was ten – it was hard to believe nobody had noticed her in all that time.

Then again, like she said yesterday, lots of people didn't really see Natalie. Maybe they thought that because she didn't speak she didn't have anything to say. The idea made me sad. Being friends with Natalie reminded me of this pencil case I used to have when I was little. It looked like a normal rectangular box, but it had lots of hidden compartments. If you pressed one button, a pencil sharpener would slide out. And, if you flicked a switch on the side, the middle part would fold in and reveal a row of coloured pens tucked underneath.

Natalie was like that – full of little surprises that you couldn't see from the outside. She was a green belt in tae kwon do. She knew British Sign Language and how to make macarons. Her favourite animals were rats, which made me shudder, but she spoke about them so passionately and showed me so many photos that I actually ended up thinking they were quite cute. She was just like that word we'd made together the first time we spoke: *unexpected.*

"It's ~~~~~~ weird, though, don't you think?" Eilidh C said suddenly.

Even though I was sitting with my back to her, I could tell her nose was wrinkling up in that way it always did when she didn't like something.

"Both the poems are made from other people's words. That's like ∼∼∼∼∼∼! Why don't they just write them?"

"I don't know. Maybe the person making them prefers it that way," said Eilidh O. "Anyway, lots of ∼∼∼∼∼∼ use spoken words in different ways."

She told everyone about the articles she'd read after she got her poem. Apparently, in certain places, people would physically give someone their words when they were making a promise to them, and in others they would say their wishes and dreams out loud, then bury the words underground in the hope they might take root. The expression 'to eat your words' had come about because, back in seventeenth-century England, people were actually made to eat their words when they were wrong.

"Well, I love it." Out of the corner of my eye, I saw Frankie's words were a firm burgundy. "Yesterday was so horrible. It's really nice that somebody, whoever they were, cared ∼∼∼∼∼∼ to do that."

"It is. I loved mine too," said Eilidh O. "I still have it on my wall at home."

"I hope I get one!" Olu said.

Scott slurped from his can of Fanta. "Me too!"

Natalie and I looked at each other. We both gave a tiny smile, so quick and small that no one watching us would even have noticed. And, although neither of us said anything, that was the moment we made the decision: we had more poems to create together.

Lots more.

Thirteen

That Saturday was my twelfth birthday. Back home in Spain, Papa and I had lots of birthday traditions. Iaia would always come round first thing, even though she hates getting up early, and I would be allowed to open all my presents over breakfast. My friends and I would come to our flat after school, and we'd play video games non-stop until dinner. And later, after everyone had gone home, Papa and I would go and buy churros from a little place round the corner. Papa liked his plain but I always got a cup of melted chocolate to dip mine into. We'd carry them down to the beach, the paper triangles warm in our hands, and sit on the edge of the promenade to eat them. If I dropped one in the sand, Papa always let me have one of his to make up for it.

We wouldn't be able to do any of that in Fortrose, and I couldn't help but feel sad about it. Papa kept saying we'd do something special, that we could 'make new traditions'. I shot down all his ideas until he suggested going to a forest adventure park just under an hour away. I'd seen adverts online, and it looked fun.

"Can I bring Natalie?" I asked.

I would have liked to invite the Eilidhs too, but there wasn't enough room for two more people in Ryan's car, and I didn't want either of them to feel left out.

"Of course!" Papa said, smiling. "You can bring anyone you like."

So on Saturday morning, after pancakes for breakfast and birthday video calls to Iaia and my friends, we drove off with Papa and Ryan in the front seats and Natalie and me squashed in with the dogs in the back. Natalie wasn't able to speak but I'd expected that – she didn't like being in unusual situations or with people she didn't know, and this was a bit of both. Plus, Ryan was her PE teacher, so he was a walking, talking reminder of school. But, since it was my birthday, Papa (who was usually a total Spotify hog) let me choose the music we listened to in the car, so Natalie and I spent most of the time passing his phone back and forth to pick songs. Celine was overexcited and yapped the whole way there, and Dion kept licking Natalie's face to make her feel welcome.

It was a cold grey February morning, but luckily the rain stopped just as we got to the park. Natalie had been there lots of times so she knew the best things to do. First up were the water slides. There were three of them, including one that was such a steep drop it almost looked like the little dinghies zipping down it would fall slap into the ground below – Natalie and I did that one four times, and every time she screamed so loudly I thought my ears would ring all day.

Ryan made Papa go on one with him while Natalie and I stayed with the dogs. When they hit the bottom, Papa got soaked with water, and his hair stuck to his forehead like seaweed. Ryan and I both laughed a lot at that.

Next we did the roller coaster, the climbing wall and the high-wire obstacle course, and then we stopped to have lunch at the park café. Natalie surprised me with a present – a notebook with drawings of palm trees on the cover because I'd told her those were one of the things I missed about home. Papa had bought me a chocolate cake shaped like a caterpillar, and Ryan had remembered to bring candles and matches, so they insisted on embarrassing me by singing 'Happy Birthday' in front of the whole café. Two other families even joined in.

"Make a wish," Papa said in English, his words the colour of toasted sugar.

Blowing out my candles, I realized I wasn't sure what to wish for. It would make sense to wish for Papa to change his mind about this place and take me back to Cadaqués, just like I'd been hoping for weeks. It had been sad having to hear Iaia sing 'Cumpleaños feliz' over the phone, and I missed my friends, and all this wasn't the same as churros on the beach.

But it had still been a really good birthday so far, maybe even one of my best. It didn't feel right to wish it away. For now I was happy where I was. Just for today.

After lunch, Papa and Ryan wanted to walk along the treetop trail through the forest. It sounded boring but was actually quite nice. The wooden walkway rose high into the trees, and you could see little birds in their nests and squirrels zipping between the branches. While Papa and Ryan dawdled behind with Dion, Natalie and I ran to keep up with Celine and kept an eye out for interesting words. Now that we'd decided we had more poems to deliver, we needed something to make them with.

There were a few good ones. I found a strawberry-coloured *love* caught between the wooden slats of the pathway and a golden *stars* fluttering on a branch. Natalie got a **universe** and a *hopefully*, but there weren't many more. They'd already been blown away in the breeze, or maybe plucked by the birds to build their nests.

"Wordsearching again?" Papa asked when he and Ryan caught up with us.

They'd seen the poem that Natalie made for me on my wall at home and asked me about it, so I'd ended up showing them my small word collection in the biscuit tin. They both seemed to think it was a bit strange, but Papa was happy that I was taking an interest in English.

"There are not so many," I said, holding up my two finds. "It makes too much wind here."

"How about we make some good ones for you then?" Ryan asked. "Like, um … *discombobulated*."

He cupped the word in his hands and held it out for me to see. Papa leaned in too, mouthing the syllables silently. "I don't know this one. What does it mean?"

"Confused," Ryan said. "As in, *I woke up feeling totally discombobulated*."

"Discom … discombub…" It took me a few tries to get it right, but eventually the word came out in bold letters and a deep purple colour. I tucked it into my pocket. "Thank you."

Ryan swung his arms and thought hard as we walked. "Oh, here's another good one: *galavanting*. It means to travel or move about, having fun."

"It is like my name!" I said as Ryan passed the word over to me. It was a sherbet-orange colour. "Gala V-anting." That one was going in my tin as soon as I got home.

"What about you, Natalie?" Papa asked. "What words do you like?"

Natalie took out her phone, typed something, then held it up to show us. On the screen was the word *gloaming*.

"That's a Scottish one," Ryan said, nodding approvingly. "It means twilight or dusk. That time after the sun goes down but before it's completely dark," he added, seeing that I didn't understand *twilight* or *dusk*, either.

He and Natalie gave me a few more to put in my pocket, and then Ryan asked Papa and me about our favourite words in Catalan.

"I like *xiuxiuejar*." I made my voice as quiet as I could. "It means talk like this."

"To whisper," Papa said, smiling. "It suits the meaning well, I think."

Ryan tried to repeat it, but it came out written **shooshooajar**. The word looked so silly that Papa and I both started laughing.

"Good try, my love," Papa said, patting Ryan's shoulder. "This one is easier – *somiatruites*. That's a daydreamer, but it literally means someone who dreams of omelettes."

Natalie pulled a face. She didn't like eggs, so a dream about omelettes would be more like a nightmare for her.

Ryan tried to say the word a few times, and each attempt came out more misshapen than the last. I was laughing lots but only because it looked and sounded funny, and I could tell from his big grin that Ryan didn't mind.

He was the sort of person who could always laugh at himself – I liked that about him.

Natalie was smiling too, but she seemed worried. When we reached the end of the path, and Papa and Ryan headed towards the café to get a coffee, she wrote something on her phone and passed it to me.

What if Mr Young tells someone at school about the words?

I felt a little kick of nerves at the thought of that, but I shook my head and smiled. "Here he is not Mr Young. He is Ryan. He will not tell someone."

Natalie nodded and put her phone in her pocket. Suddenly she gave a gasp and pointed to the trees behind me. I spun round and looked up but couldn't see anything except leaves and branches. By the time I turned back, Natalie had darted ahead, grinning at me over her shoulder as she ran. I laughed and chased after her. Our footsteps shook the wooden walkway as we raced through the forest.

Fourteen

Natalie and I created and delivered three new poems the following week. One went to Alice Thompson, who had talked about her anxiety in her English class – Natalie knew a lot about that. One was for Nicky Poplawski, after Craig had laughed at him in PE – Natalie knew how that felt too. And the third was called *Sunflower* and was for Olu, just to thank her for always being so nice to everyone. Natalie left it in the spot on the second-floor corridor where she and the others always sat during break, in a pink envelope with her name on it. Olu was so pleased when she found it, she did a happy dance.

We sent another three poems the next week, and then four, and soon it seemed like every single person in first year had heard about our project. Every morning in registration, there was a buzz about who might find today's anonymous message, and lots of first years who'd never used their lockers before started checking them as soon as they got to school. I even spotted a few second years peeking into theirs, as if hoping that they might find a poem too.

All the while, I kept looking out for clues about who else might need a little bit of hope. I was beginning to realize that there was a lot you could learn about someone without even talking to them, just by paying attention and reading their body language. Like how hard Leonie was fighting to stay best friends with Amy, who was gravitating towards other people, and how sad she was about it. And how Ross, who always made jokes and pretended that he didn't care when he got a bad mark on a test or for his homework, actually tried really hard at school and had to hide his disappointment when he didn't do well.

Soon our list of people to write poems for was so long that our combined word collections weren't big enough to cover them. Natalie and I even started waiting around after school and sneaking handfuls of words from the big blue bins that the cleaners swept them into at the end of the day, just to have enough to make them all. My head was constantly swirling with new English words:

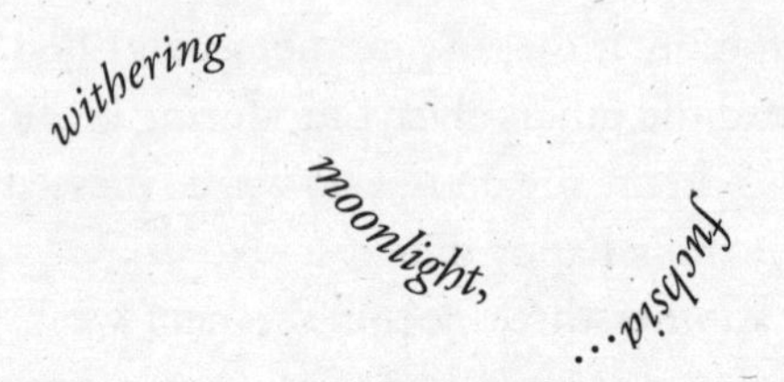

Entire constellations of words mapped out in my mind like stars. It made my brain hurt but it was worth it when I got to see someone find one of the poems.

Hiding them was usually my job since it made Natalie too anxious. Sometimes I had to get really creative – once I spilled a packet of Skittles all over the floor in Art so I could bend down and slip a note into Katie King's pocket while everyone was busy picking them up. Afterwards,

I tried to keep an eye on Katie across the classroom, but was distracted by Eilidh C talking to me.

"∼∼∼∼∼∼ ∼∼∼∼∼∼ ∼∼∼∼∼∼, you know?" she whispered. Eilidh O had gone to the dentist, so it was just me and Eilidh C at our table. "But I ∼∼∼∼∼∼ ∼∼∼∼∼∼ ∼∼∼∼∼∼."

I had no idea what she was saying. Eilidh C always spoke quickly, and today her words were falling so fast it looked like ribbons were spilling from her lips. The strangest thing was their colour. Her speech usually came out in very bold, vivid shades, but today it was watery blue.

"Yes," I said, stealing another glance at Katie as I shaded in my drawing.

Katie was a very quiet, shy girl who I'd found crying in the toilets twice since I started school. Neither Natalie nor I knew why, but she clearly needed cheering up, so we'd made a poem for her called *Every Cloud.*

Eilidh said something else then but Mrs Fraser told us to stop chatting and get on with our work.

The rest of the lesson passed, and Katie still hadn't found the note. Then, as we were leaving the classroom, she reached into her pocket and pulled it out. Olu and Frankie came out of the classroom opposite ours with Natalie a few steps behind them. Olu's eyes lit up when she saw the paper in Katie's hand.

"Is that another poem, Katie? Can we see?"

In just a few seconds, a crowd of eight or nine people had gathered round Katie. Her face went bright red but she smiled as she handed the piece of paper over to Olu. I caught Natalie's eye, and we exchanged tiny smiles before leaning in to read the words that we had put together yesterday.

Every **cloud** **is** **stitched** *with* **silver**,

Beneath **the** ***dirt***, there's ***sometimes*** *gold* –

Suddenly the paper flew out of Olu's fingers. We all spun round: Craig was jogging backwards down the corridor, the page in his hand and a wide smirk on his face. He read out the poem in a loud, high-pitched voice as he moved, all the letters pulled out of shape from his mocking. Beside me, Natalie's hands clenched into fists.

Frankie ran down the corridor and snatched the poem back. "Shut up, Craig," they snapped. "It's Katie's."

"OK, OK." Craig held his hands up, like he hadn't done anything, and Frankie was the one being unreasonable. "I think it's creepy but whatever."

The word ***creepy*** stuck on the collar of his shirt. I didn't know what the word meant, but judging by the sickly green tone it wasn't anything good.

"It's not creepy," Katie said quietly as Frankie handed the poem back to her. "I love it."

She looked down at the paper and smiled. It was a soft, warm smile, and it made me flush with pride. Natalie had done most of the work putting the poem together, but I had helped – I'd suggested the word **cloud** after it fell out of a Geography textbook, which gave her the idea for the first line.

"Honestly, I agree with Craig." Eilidh C's face was scrunched up like she'd smelled something bad. "It *is* pretty weird. It looks like a ransom note."

"What are you talking about?" Olu said as Natalie started

looking up pictures of ransom notes on her phone to show me what that meant. "It's not weird at all. It's really nice!"

"Craig just tries to 〰〰〰 everything that makes anyone happy." Frankie rolled their eyes. "It's because he's a sad, miserable person."

Miserable. That word existed in Catalan and Spanish too. It sounded different in English but maybe it meant the same thing.

"Craig is miserable?" I asked.

"Probably." Olu shrugged. "Why else would he be such a 〰〰〰?"

I missed the word but I could guess what Olu had meant – I'd heard Craig called lots of things since I started school, not many of them good. Even so, I thought about what Olu and Frankie said all the way to our next class. Maybe something had happened in Craig's life to make him such a bully. Maybe he needed someone to tell him that things would get better too.

Now that our waiting list had become so long, Natalie and I decided that I'd go to her house at the weekend to keep working on the poems. When I got there after lunch on Saturday, there were lots of banging sounds and loud voices coming from upstairs.

"Burst pipe in the bathroom," Natalie said when she opened the door. She had Ava in her right arm, her wooden box of words tucked under the left, and a bag of carrot sticks in her hand. "I said we'd stay out here in the garden while Mum and Charlie sort it out."

"Yes, of course." The sun was out for the first time in

weeks, and I wanted to make the most of every minute of it.

I waved at Ava, who was chewing on her soft toy giraffe's very soggy ear. "I like your friend, Ava. What is his name?"

"Name," said Ava slowly. I wasn't sure if she was just repeating what I was saying or if that was what the toy was called.

Natalie laughed. "She's called Giraphaella, but Avie just calls her Raffey."

She set her sister down on the grass, carefully retrieved the word **name** from the folds in Ava's dungarees and popped it in her box.

"Have you decided what you're going to do with your collection yet?" she asked me.

"No, still not." I'd used lots of the words that I'd collected to help make poems, but others had already faded away.

"Well, there's no rush. You can always start a new one when you move home."

It felt strange to think about looking for words in Cadaqués. There must be people who did it there, and everywhere else in the world too. I sometimes wondered if any of the kids in my old class had been wordsearchers like us, and I just hadn't noticed. But, for me, collecting words was tied up with Fortrose and Natalie and learning English. I couldn't picture myself doing it in Cadaqués the way I did here.

"So." Natalie took her notebook from the back pocket of her jeans and opened it to a new page. "Who do we want to write for next?"

There was an idea that had been bouncing round my head for a few days. "You will think this is weird, but maybe … Craig?"

Natalie paused to wipe Ava's nose with a hankie. "Craig? You mean Craig Miller? Why him of all people?"

"You remember what I told you? Frankie and Olu said that Craig is very miserable. Maybe this is why he is so horrible."

Part of me felt bad for suggesting it. Craig was so mean to Natalie, and for no reason other than he could be. It wasn't like he was jealous of her being so smart – he was in the top sets for Maths and English, and he was good at sports and gaming too. He was only nasty to her because she was different, and he knew he could get away with it. Now that I felt more confident in English, I'd started speaking up. I'd told him to shut up after he made a nasty comment about her hair in the library a few days ago, but he'd just laughed and ignored me.

"Maybe." Natalie gently pulled a daisy out of Ava's mouth. "But I don't think Craig deserves a poem."

"You are right," I said quickly, seeing the blueish tone that was leaking into her words. "He does not deserve one word from you. Not even a really, really small word like *a* or *to*. Forget it. I said nothing."

Natalie smiled. "You know, he was different in primary school. He was always really loud, and he made a lot of jokes, but he wasn't a bully like he is now. He wasn't a total –" she looked at Ava and seemed to remember that she wasn't supposed to say bad words in front of her little sister – "bag of baby poop."

I giggled. "He is the most big bag of baby poop in the world."

"The biggest in the universe. But … maybe, if we're nice to him, he might become, like, a medium-sized bag of baby poop." She sighed so hard it sent some of her words scurrying across the grass. "OK. He's probably just going to say it's weird and laugh at it, but whatever. Let's do it."

Ava was starting to whinge, so I took her on my lap and fed her carrot sticks while Natalie picked out words and placed them in her notebook. The poem took her a little longer than usual, but eventually she passed it to me to read.

"Let's call it *Echo*," she said.

She caught the word as it fell from her mouth. It was a rich aubergine colour. She set it at the top of the page and gently patted it with her cloth.

"What do you think?"

"I like it," I said. "What do you think, Ava?"

"**CARROT!**" Ava shouted, big and green.

I shouted it too, which made her burst into giggles and clap her hands. Laughing, Natalie picked up her baby sister's brand-new word and slipped it into the box, ready to be saved forever in Ava's book.

Craig didn't make fun of our poem. In fact, he didn't say anything about it at all. Whenever we'd delivered the other poems, we'd always heard people discussing them a few hours later. This time, days went by, and no one brought up Craig's note. I even peeked through the slats of his locker trying to see if he'd missed it – there was a whole term's worth of empty crisp packets and detention slips in there, but the poem seemed to be gone.

It was strange but Natalie and I were too busy with our next poems to think much about Craig. That week, we hid a couple every day, under computer keyboards and in textbooks, and even taped one to the goalposts on the football pitch. We were so busy that sometimes whole days would go by when I hardly thought about my plan to make Papa move home, or about Cadaqués at all.

But the following Wednesday something went very wrong.

I sensed it as soon as I walked into registration that morning. There was a cluster of kids huddled round Caitlin Mackay's desk, including the Eilidhs, and the atmosphere felt strange. Ms Anderson hadn't arrived yet, so I joined the group and tugged on Eilidh O's sleeve.

"What is it?" I asked.

"Caitlin got one of those poems, but it's different..." Eilidh O's eyebrows were knitted in a frown. "It's really mean. Not like the others at all."

My stomach flipped. Natalie and I hadn't written a poem for Caitlin yet, but she was holding a lined piece of paper with words pressed on to it, just like ours. For a second I wondered if Natalie had done it without telling me. I moved behind Eilidh C so I could see the poem.

It's ***raining***, it's *pouring*,

Caitlin Mackay is ***BORING***.

She *sucks* at French, she *sucks* at Maths,

And she *really sucks* at **DRAWING**.

My mouth went dry. This hadn't come from Natalie. Her poems were much better than whatever this was, but, more importantly, she wouldn't write something so nasty. Not even to Craig or Abigail, and definitely not for Caitlin. She was a loud, talkative girl who giggled a lot and was constantly doodling – she'd draw on jotters, textbooks, her friends' schoolbags and hands. Now her cheeks were bright red, and her eyes were glassy from trying not to cry.

"Well, somebody ~~~~~~ hates me." Caitlin forced a laugh. The words came out so wobbly it looked like she was talking through an earthquake. "I don't suck at drawing, do I?"

"Of course you don't," Eilidh O said quickly. "You're amazing at drawing."

"You're not boring, either," Leonie said in a firm terracotta colour. "And *boring* and *drawing* don't even rhyme properly!"

Ms Anderson came into the room then, so everyone started moving back to their own seats. Caitlin scrunched the paper into a tight ball and flicked it on to the floor. Ross picked it up and threw it towards the bin, then punched the air when it hit the rim and bounced inside.

"Why does someone do this?" I whispered to the Eilidhs as we sat down at our desks by the window. "The other poems … they are not like this."

"I have no idea," said Eilidh O. "It's really odd."

Eilidh C's eyes narrowed at me. For one horrible moment I was sure she was going to accuse me of making it, but then she shrugged. "It's probably just somebody playing a prank. That means a joke," she added to me, smiling.

"Well, it's not funny." Eilidh O's words were a deep shade of red that I hadn't seen from her before. "Poor Caitlin."

My stomach felt jittery all morning, and when the bell rang for breaktime I practically sprinted down the corridor to find Natalie. She looked at me with big, startled eyes, and I knew she'd already heard about the poem. I grabbed her arm, and we hurried outside to our spot around the back of the gym.

"Who do you think did it?" Natalie whispered.

I took my chocolate sandwich from my bag, but didn't unwrap the foil. I still felt too unsettled to eat. "Do you know somebody who hates Caitlin?"

"I know she and Rachel had a big falling-out just after Christmas, but they're friends again now." Natalie had a cereal bar in her hand but she hadn't touched it, either. "Can you remember what the poem actually said about her?"

All that had stuck with me was something about Caitlin being boring and bad at drawing. It didn't mention anything that she'd said or done. It was just mean for the sake of being mean – and that made me think of someone in particular.

"Craig? He said nothing about our poem. Maybe he did not like it, and it gave him the idea to do this."

It didn't seem likely. Craig didn't need to be sneaky to make nasty comments – he did it to people's faces every day. But Natalie nodded. "That's what I was thinking too. We can keep an eye on him on the trip tomorrow. Caitlin as well."

The next day everyone in our year was going to a castle for a History field trip. We could watch out for anything Craig might say or do to give himself away, and look out for anyone making comments about Caitlin or giving her nasty looks. Our poems were special – they had made people happy, and they'd given me and Natalie another way to communicate with our classmates. We couldn't let this anonymous person, whoever they were, spoil that for us.

Sixteen

The atmosphere in registration the next morning reminded me of school-trip days back home. Everyone was happy and noisy, excited to swap classes for a day at the castle. We were allowed to wear our normal clothes and just seeing everyone in their own colours put me in a good mood. It took me so long to pick my outfit, though, that I realized part of me liked our uniform now – it was much easier not to have to choose something to wear every morning. I'd eventually settled on my favourite jeans, purple trainers and a jumper with alpacas on it, which Eilidh O said she loved.

After the bell rang, three buses arrived to take all the first years to the castle. Craig raced towards the middle one with his friends, shouting something about the back seat. I hurried after them, the Eilidhs right behind me, and saved a spot for Natalie a few rows in front of Craig. We were quiet for a moment after she arrived, trying to pick out his conversation from the chatter around us.

"What does he say?" I whispered as the bus pulled away from school.

It was still hard for me to understand what people were

talking about if I couldn't see them to read the words or their lips. Some of Craig's words came bouncing

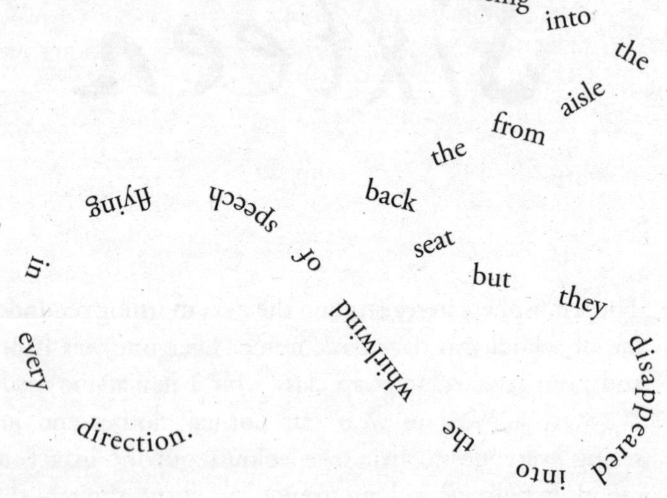

Natalie took out her phone to answer me.

They're just making fun of Luke for crying at a TV show. Nothing about the poem yet.

Soon Ross persuaded the driver to let him put a playlist on, and it got too noisy to hear what Craig was saying at all. Caitlin was on the same bus, so he might not have mentioned the poem with her here anyway. With nothing else to investigate, Natalie and I opened the packet of lentil chips that her mum had given her and played a game on my phone together until we arrived at the castle.

When it finally came into view, I gasped. It was an enormous cream-coloured building with long, pointy turrets and an immaculate green garden of perfectly trimmed hedges, colourful flower beds and marble statues around a large pond that sparkled in the sunshine. I instantly whipped out my phone to take photos for Iaia – it looked just like the sets of the cheesy period dramas she loved so much.

The buses pulled up in the car park, and the teachers ushered us towards the castle's ornate front doors. Natalie and I fell in line just behind Craig and his friends, but then he grabbed Luke's hat and sprinted up the steps to the castle until Miss Shah told him to stop running. She and a few other teachers had come along to help out. Today she was wearing sparkly parrot earrings and a matching red-and-blue cardigan.

"Hi, girls." She waved when she saw Natalie and me climbing the steps. "Quite impressive, huh? It's as big as, well, a castle!"

I grinned. We'd learned about similes in Miss Shah's class yesterday. "As pretty as a … parakeet," I added, inspired by her earrings.

Miss Shah laughed and shook her head to make the parrots jingle. "Good one."

Behind its big wooden doors, the castle was just as flamboyant as it looked from the outside: a huge marble stairway leading up to a stone archway with dozens of old swords criss-crossing beneath the ceiling. The teachers moved us all to one side of the hallway, and Mr Calvin gave a short talk about the place before we went inside. I was too busy looking around to follow most of it, but I got that the main building was around 300 years old and that Queen Victoria had once stayed here. After that, Miss Shah handed out a list of items that we had to find around the castle and some questions about them.

"Sort yourselves into groups of four," said Mr Calvin. "There'll be a prize for the team that hands in all the right answers first, so get a move on!"

Natalie and I joined up with the Eilidhs. Eilidh C didn't look too happy about being in the same group as Natalie, or vice versa, but Frankie, Olu, Scott and Amina had already formed another team.

"Let's start in the museum." Eilidh O pointed at the list. "There's a ∼∼∼∼∼∼ stone on the list. That's got to be in there."

She led us into a large room lined with glass display cabinets filled with different objects that previous owners of the castle had collected over the years. Lots of them had obviously been stolen from other countries, like the pretty turquoise Islamic jugs and some ancient daggers from Kenya – we all agreed those should be given back right away. But there were some interesting things from Scotland, like the Pictish stones that Eilidh O was looking for. They turned out to be large slabs of rock with Celtic patterns etched into them, some created as long ago as the fifth century. The question said we had to copy the pattern, so I leaned on Eilidh C's back and drew it as best I could.

"Good." She nodded, inspecting my work. Eilidh C was super competitive, and she really wanted to win Mr Calvin's mystery prize. "Let's do the gold-panning question next."

She and Eilidh O dashed over to a display at the other end of the room, but Natalie tapped me on the shoulder. She pointed at something inside one of the glass cabinets. Tucked away behind a collection of old cups and plates was a scrap of yellowing paper with four lines of text on it.

"These are spoken words!" I cried.

I cast a quick glance around me, but luckily our classmates were busy with the quiz and didn't seem to have heard my loud coppery words.

Miss Shah looked up from the miniature statues that she'd been studying. "People used speech like that a lot in the olden days," she said, walking over to join us. "They would press their words one by one on to paper, or wood, or slate before paper was available, and use them to send messages. Like that, see?"

She pointed to another object behind the glass: a large slab of grey stone with pale yellow words pasted on to it. I leaned so close my nose was almost touching the glass but the words were so faded I couldn't make out what they said. I wondered how people back then made the words stick to the stone, since they wouldn't have silk cloths like Natalie.

"Why have they stopped?" I asked Miss Shah.

"Well, as more people started going to school, and paper and ink became more readily available in Europe, using saved speech became a sign of illiteracy. That means not knowing how to read and write," she told me, talking in slow, clear green. "People would make fun of those who used words like this because they thought they were uneducated, and eventually it became seen as something shameful, and it died out. There's still a stigma around it today."

So that was why seeing Natalie wordsearching had felt so strange to me at first. The thought made me sad – all those people having one of their ways to communicate taken away from them.

"It was different in other countries, of course," said Miss Shah. "Lots of cultures still place a great deal of importance on oral storytelling and the spoken word, as well as writing. There's no one right or wrong way to do things."

What Miss Shah said was interesting, but complicated too. It was only when she walked away that I realized that I'd understood almost every sentence, and I hadn't needed to translate them in my head at all. There were loads of words I didn't recognize but they still slotted into place, exactly like when I listened to people speak Catalan or Spanish.

I felt a sudden burst of pride. The Gala who had arrived here in January and gone hours and hours without saying a single word seemed like a different person now. I grinned at Natalie, put my hands on her shoulders and steered her over to join the Eilidhs. They'd completed another three questions, and Eilidh O was already practising her victory dance.

After the museum, we moved to the drawing room and the library, which were filled with mahogany furniture, ornate gold-framed mirrors and portraits of people who had lived there generations ago. Caitlin was in one of the rooms with her group, so I kept an eye on them as Eilidh C filled in the questions on our answer sheet. If Caitlin was still upset about the poem, it didn't show – she and Rachel were giggling hysterically at a painting of a man posing with a huge fish.

We spent another hour or so on the quiz and then were sent out into the gardens to eat our packed lunches. Natalie, the Eilidhs and I sat down on a picnic bench with Frankie, Olu, Scott and Amina. Ryan had been in charge of making my lunch box since Papa had gone to Inverness for an interview early this morning, and he hadn't done a bad job: a salmon-and-cream-cheese bagel, prawn cocktail crisps, a nectarine, and one of my favourite strawberry tarts.

"Ooh, is that from the bakery on the high street?" Olu asked, leaning over the bench to peer into my lunch box. "I love those."

"Take a piece." I tried to split the tart in two but the pastry disintegrated and I ended up with cream and strawberry sauce all over my fingers. Olu laughed and wrinkled her nose.

"No thanks. Think I'll pass."

I pretended to pout. "Why? You don't want my germens?"

"I think you mean *germs*," Eilidh O giggled. "Not Germans."

"No, no, I mean Germans," I said seriously, licking the cream from my fingers. "This strawberry is from Berlin. His name is Hans."

They all laughed. Even Eilidh C, who was still in a huff after Mr Calvin announced that Katie King's group had come first in the quiz, grinned and rolled her eyes. "You're so weird, Gala."

I shoved part of the tart into my mouth and grinned. I'd missed being able to do this – shaping my words into jokes and silliness and making people laugh at them, like a clown twisting balloons into different animals. It reminded me of being with Pau and Laia and Mariam and my other friends back home. I felt a twinge of homesickness as I thought of them, but only a small one.

After lunch, we had time to visit the gift shop, where Eilidh O and I spent so long posing and taking pictures of each other in silly tartan hats that we forgot to buy anything. Then we were led back outside for a falconry display. The castle grounds were home to three falcons and two hawks, and a member of staff showed us how people used them to hunt with back in the day. Natalie and I stood right behind Craig and Abigail so we could listen in on their conversation, but I got distracted by the birds soaring and swooping round us and forgot all about our investigation.

Before I knew it, it was two o'clock and we were being shepherded back on to the buses. I asked Natalie if she'd heard Craig say anything about Caitlin or the poem, but she shook her head.

Maybe we'll never know, she wrote on her phone, shrugging.

But the curiosity still itched at me. "You do not want to try? I need to know who wrote that!"

Me too but we don't have any clues or any evidence, Natalie typed. It's probably best to forget about it.

Most of us had left our jackets on the buses since it was sunny, so the teachers told us to sit in the same seats. Craig, Abigail and their friends raced to the back again. Luke was leading the way but he stopped so suddenly that Craig bumped into him.

"What's that?" Luke asked, pointing to something on the seat.

He picked up a folded piece of paper with one word written on it. Abigail snatched it from him and opened the note. After a moment, she turned round and scanned the bus. Her cheeks had gone pink.

"Who left this here?" she shouted.

No one answered. Craig pulled the paper out of her hand. Abigail made a grab for it but he ducked under Luke's arm and began clambering over the seats to get away from her.

"Hickory dickory dock," Craig read out, his words coming out in big green letters. "Abigail's teeth are like broken rocks."

He stopped reading just as Abigail grabbed the poem out of his hand. There was a ripping sound as the piece of paper tore in two. Abigail's face was now scarlet, and her eyes were bright. I didn't know what a 'hickory' or a 'dickory' was, but she clearly wasn't happy to be called either.

"Come on, who wrote this? My teeth aren't even that bad!" she shouted, her words the same shade of pink as her skin.

She added a bunch of words that made Mr Calvin shout a large scarlet, "Abigail Hislop!" and give her a day's detention. Craig and Luke had been sniggering but they stopped when Abigail flopped down on to the seat beside them. She looked like she was about to cry.

"Nah, that's ~~~~~~, though," Luke said awkwardly.

"Yeah. If you're going to say that, say it to her face. Like I do," Craig added, elbowing Abigail in the ribs. She laughed, but she put her hand up to cover her mouth as she did so.

Twisting round in my seat, I looked at Natalie. Her eyes were dark. She gave me a short, serious nod, a silent pact to keep investigating. Forgetting about it was no longer an option.

Seventeen

Whoever was writing the nasty messages had clearly been busy. When I got to school the next day, I saw a group of girls by reception surrounding Jayne Harris, who was clutching a piece of lined paper and crying. I carried on down the corridor and found a small crowd gathered round the lockers. A piece of paper was taped to one of them, until Ben Dupont pushed through the crowd and pulled it down. His face turned red as he looked at the poem.

"Which ~~~~~~ put this here?" he shouted.

No one answered. Ben ripped the paper, shoved the pieces into his pocket and squeezed back through the crowd again. The floor was littered with hushed words and whispers, and they swirled round my feet as I hurried to registration. My stomach felt jittery, and when I walked through the door to 1C, my heart sank even further. Eilidh C was sitting at her desk with her head down and a piece of white paper in her hands.

"You too?" I whispered, slumping into my seat.

Eilidh C looked at me with steely eyes. She spoke in small, tight words the same pale grey as the sky outside. "Why, who else got one?"

I told her about the poems that had been left for Jayne and Ben. Eilidh O was frowning at the piece of paper. I twisted my head to the side to read the words. They said something about *wall* and *fall*, but I only managed to read the first couple of lines before Eilidh C crumpled the page up.

"It's making fun of me for being tall," she said, rolling her eyes. "Really original."

"It's based on another nursery rhyme," Eilidh O said. "What do you think that means?"

I glanced from the poem to her sherbet-orange words, which had fallen on to her desk. "What are nursery rhymes?"

"Little songs or poems for babies," Eilidh O said. "This one's based on a poem called *Humpty Dumpty*. Caitlin's one was from *It's Raining, It's Pouring*, and Abigail's was *Hickory Dickory Dock*."

"The person probably just found a book and copied them," said Eilidh C. "Maybe they have a wee brother or sister."

There was something strange about the way she was talking. Eilidh C's voice sounded angry, but I'd seen her angry before, and her words always became bolder and sharper then. Now they were pale, and the spacing between the letters was smaller than usual. Maybe she was more upset by the note than she wanted us to see. People's speech could look completely different depending on their emotions. Sometimes so different it was hard to recognize as theirs.

The atmosphere felt tense and strange when we headed to Friday assembly. Natalie had saved me a seat in the second row, like she always did. I sat down beside her and held up three fingers.

"More poems!" I whispered. "Jayne, Ben and Eilidh C."

Natalie's eyes widened, but before I could tell her anything else Mr Watson cleared his throat and started talking. Friday assemblies were always difficult for me to follow – there was so much *talking*, though sometimes the choir would sing a song or the drama group would act out a scene from the show they were working on.

Today Mr Watson spoke about a Maths competition and the French exchange that the third years were going on in May, but I took in even less than usual. All I could think of were the poems, and Jayne crying, and Eilidh C's misshapen words, and the look on Ben's face when he'd ripped the poem in two. Who would want to do that to them? And why?

"Finally," said Mr Watson, "it's been brought to my 〰〰〰 that several first-year students have been sent some rather 〰〰〰 notes recently."

I jumped – it was almost as if he'd seen inside my head. Mr Watson held up a lined piece of paper. I leaned forward to make sure I could read the dark grey words coming from his mouth.

"They seem to be made out of speech, and they make hurtful comments about the people they have been sent to. This is bullying and will not be tolerated. When we find out who did this, they'll be punished."

He placed the note back on the lectern and scanned the front rows of the hall, where the first years were sitting.

"In the meantime, I don't want to see anyone collecting spoken words. Not for any reason at all. Is that understood?"

A shower of quiet *yes, sir*s fell to the floor. My heart skipped a beat, and beside me Natalie flinched. There were words in my pocket that I'd picked up this morning – a fern-green ***understand***, said by Papa while he was on the phone to someone yesterday, and a shimmering lilac *eternity* that I'd found stuck to a lamp post on my way to school. Now they felt like little grenades, ready to explode and get us into trouble.

When everyone stood up to leave the hall, I slid my hand into my pocket to grab the words, took a quick look around to make sure no one was watching me, then let them drop to the floor. I grabbed Natalie's hand, hurried down the corridor and pulled her into the girls' toilets by reception. Luckily we were the only ones inside.

"What do we do?" I whispered. "We have to discover who is doing this."

Natalie was chewing on her thumbnail. She looked scared and sad. Wordsearching was such a big part of who she was. She glanced down at all the words covering the bathroom floor. Words that would be swept up and dissolve into nothing in a few days, weeks or months.

"But … I don't want to stop," she said, her words dark blue and tiny. "I can't."

I could tell what she was thinking – that she had managed to keep her collection secret for years, and there was no reason why that should change just because Mr Watson said so. Normally I'd agree. The rule was unfair, and it made no sense – whoever was making these poems didn't need to wordsearch at school when there was endless speech outside for them to pick from. But I didn't want anyone to catch us and think we were responsible for the poems, so I put my arm on her sleeve and shook my head.

"We have to," I whispered. "For a little bit. We find who did this, and then we can start again. OK?"

Natalie nodded. I stuck out my pinkie finger and she linked hers round it to make a promise. Whatever happened, we were in this together.

Eighteen

Ryan waited for me at the school gates after my last class that afternoon. He'd done that a few times now. At first I'd found it annoying and embarrassing, but now I quite liked it. He'd tell me about funny things that had happened in his classes during the day and try out the Catalan phrases he'd learned on his app recently. He was actually getting a lot better. He'd started watching a TV show set in a hospital for practice, and he kept trying to squeeze random medical words into our everyday conversations. That morning he'd asked me to pass him a 'scalpel' to butter his toast.

"Netball's been cancelled," he told me now, waving to some third-year kids who were yelling goodbye to him from across the courtyard. "Do you fancy a strawberry tart?"

My stomach growled before I could even think about it. I'd bought a slice of pizza at lunch but a group of kids sitting at the table opposite ours had been talking loudly about who might have left today's trio of horrible poems, and it had made me too nervous to eat anything, even though neither my name nor Natalie's was brought up.

"Yes, please," I said. "I could eat a house."

Ryan smiled. "The saying is 'I could eat a horse' but,

if you want to eat a house, go ahead. Might be a bit tough to chew, though."

We debated which would be the easiest parts of a house to eat (curtains, carpets) and the hardest (windows, fireplaces) as we walked up the road to the bakery. At the counter, Ryan asked for three strawberry tarts.

"Only two. Papa does not like those, remember?" I told him.

The last time we came here, Papa had asked for a sourdough loaf. That was his idea of a fun treat! I was just like him in so many ways, but my sweet tooth was not one of them.

Ryan smiled as the lady behind the counter slid over the box. "He might change his mind. Do you want yours now?"

My stomach rumbled again to say yes. Ryan took two from the box and we ate them as we walked down the hill towards his house. I nibbled the crust, ate the cream and left the strawberries for last. Ryan scoffed his down in three bites. It was another way he was a lot like Dion.

"So," he said, wiping cream from his mouth, "do you and Natalie know anything about those poems Mr Watson ~~~~~~~ at assembly today?"

I spun round to look at him. "It wasn't us! Well, we wrote some of them, but only the nice ones for Eilidh O and Frankie and some others, not these mean ones that have appeared lately. I have no idea who's been writing those."

In their rush to come out, the words slipped over my tongue and flew from my lips in panicked amber Catalan. Ryan told me to slow down and explain again.

"I didn't think you and Natalie would do something like that," he said afterwards, his words a calm blue.

"But do you know who did? Do lots of kids in your class collect words like that?"

"No. I do not see anyone do it," I continued in English. "Only Natalie. But we think maybe someone has copied our idea."

"It sounds like it. Strange." Ryan was frowning. "You won't keep collecting words at school, will you? Not now that Mr Watson has banned it."

I shook my head. "No, we promise to stop."

"OK, good. You can still do it at home, obviously. Outside school too."

We'd reached the house now but Ryan paused at the front door.

"I can give you some more for your collection if you want. Like … *superdisflunctuous*."

He caught the word in his hand. It was small and shiny pink. "What does it mean?" I asked.

"No idea – I just made it up."

I grinned and gave him a light shove. "Thank you very much. Now you make me even more confused."

Something felt different as soon as we stepped into the house. The dogs didn't come running out to greet me like they usually did, and people were talking in the front room. When I followed Ryan inside, I realized why he'd bought three strawberry tarts instead of two. Sitting on the sofa, with a surprisingly serene Celine in her lap and Dion slumped across her feet, was –

"*IAIA!*" Her name bounced out of my mouth in huge, sparkling gold letters. I dropped my bag and ran towards her. "What are you doing here?"

"I came to see you, of course." She laughed as I threw

myself at her in a hug. Her arms wrapped tight round me, and she kissed the side of my head three times. "Surprise!"

It felt strange seeing her in Ryan's house. She'd had her short grey hair done, and she was dressed in a white jumper and floral leggings, the big pink coat she always wore hanging over the arm of the sofa. She looked so colourful and out of place here, as if someone had cut her out of a fashion magazine and pasted her on to a black-and-white newspaper.

"You should have told me you were coming!" I said, settling down on the sofa beside her. Celine gave an annoyed yap but shuffled over to make room for me. "How long are you staying for?"

"Until next Saturday." I must have pulled a face because Iaia laughed and pinched my cheek. "What's wrong, chicken? Is that too long or not long enough?"

"Not long enough, obviously!"

"Don't worry. I've got everything I need to cook all your favourites in a week: fideuà and canelons and…" Iaia stopped and looked me up and down. "Though it seems like you've been eating well enough here. You're almost as tall as me now!"

"Too many strawberry tarts," Papa said, laughing. Ryan perched on the armrest beside him and said that was his fault.

"Oh really? Well, you won't want any of this then, Gala…" Iaia opened her big pink suitcase and began pulling out all the snacks that I'd told her I missed. There were packets of barbecue-flavour sunflower seeds, tubs of Cola Cao powder, giant puffed corn, mini chorizo and fuet sausages, and lots and lots and *lots* of chocolates and crisps.

"Thanks so much, Iaia!" I said, grabbing a big packet

of white chocolate Huesitos. I thought Papa would start going on about not eating too many sweets before dinner, but he grinned and reached for a packet of sunflower seeds. He'd kept complaining that the ones he found in the supermarkets here just weren't the same.

While I counted out the snacks, working out how long the stash could last me if I rationed it properly, Iaia updated us on some drama from her padel club and the feminist book group she'd joined. Afterwards, Papa and Ryan went to make dinner while I showed Iaia my room, and we played video games until the food was ready. She'd got even worse since Christmas, so I let her win a couple of times.

We ate at nine o'clock that night, like we would at home, and Ryan only complained twice about how hungry he was. Afterwards, he and Papa went out to the pub, and I stayed up with Iaia to watch the latest episode of a Spanish fashion reality show that we were addicted to on her tablet. We're both the kind of people who like to comment on everything when we watch movies or TV shows – it drives Papa mad – and soon our clothes, the sofa, the carpet and even the dogs were covered with our words. I picked up an *increïble* that Iaia had said. She'd been talking about the ridiculous outfit that one of the contestants had made, and the letters still hummed with her laughter.

"What are you doing with that, chicken?" she asked me.

"I've started collecting them," I told her, tucking the word into my pocket. "My friend Natalie and I do it."

An uncomfortable feeling came over me as I remembered the nasty poems and the fact that Mr Watson had banned wordsearching. With all the excitement of Iaia's arrival, I hadn't thought about it since I got home. I brushed the discomfort away and instead told Iaia about Natalie's huge collection of words and how she used them to create new things.

"She sounds like an interesting girl, this Natalie," Iaia said, smiling. "I'm glad you've made friends here. It sounds like you're settling in really well."

Her words took me by surprise. For my first few months here I'd been so focused on eventually going home that I'd actively tried *not* to settle in. But thinking about it now… I had, really. I was getting on well with Ryan again. I still missed my old friends but I wasn't thinking about them all the time any more. Speaking English was still hard, although it didn't exhaust me as much as before. The things that I liked about this place had crept up on me, and now my list looked something like this:

The best things about:

Fortrose	Cadaqués
Celine and Dion. Natalie (and Ava). The Eilidhs, Frankie, Olu, Amina and Scott. Pizza day in the canteen. The way my footsteps crunch on the grass on frosty mornings. My English lessons with Miss Shah. Walks to the Point, even if we never see these mysterious dolphins! Prawn cocktail crisps. The red squirrel that sometimes appears in the back garden. Strawberry tarts.	Everything else.

The realization left a strange feeling in my stomach. I'd missed Iaia loads since we left, and she must have missed us too. She had lots of friends, and she was always busy – as well as playing padel, she was in an amateur theatre group, and she was always trying out new classes. But she'd lived alone since my Iaio died. Papa was her only son, and I was her only grandchild. It must have felt lonely not having us around. Now that she was here and not a face on my phone screen, I remembered how much we were missing out on by being so far away.

"It's not the same," I said quickly. "This might not be forever anyway. Papa still hasn't found a job yet."

"Oh, don't worry about that." Iaia patted my knee. "I'm sure he will soon. He's getting lots of interviews."

"Maybe." I stifled a yawn. I wasn't used to staying up this late any more. "Well, at least we still have the flat. Just in case we do decide to go back."

Iaia opened her mouth to reply, then held back the words. Instead she pointed at the tablet screen, where one of the fashion designers was making a hat so big you could fit an entire football team underneath it. "Look what she's doing now! Do you think I could pull off a hat like that?"

I laughed and curled up against the cushions. "Oh yeah. Definitely."

Nineteen

A weekend with Iaia was exactly what I needed to take my mind off the mystery messages. We ate, laughed, went for walks and drives to show her the area, ate some more, laughed some more, and watched around eight episodes of our reality show together. But, even so, I walked into registration on Monday with a rugby-sized ball of nerves in my stomach, waiting to find another flurry of mean poems.

Luckily there didn't seem to be any, or at least not in our registration class. By the time the bell rang at the end of Geography, I hadn't heard about any new messages and was finally starting to relax. The person had written five whole poems – maybe they'd run out of words or nursery rhymes to plagiarize, and that would *finally* be the end of this whole strange ordeal.

But a few minutes after I sat down in Music there was a knock on the door. A second-year boy who I recognized from the canteen came in with a message for Mrs Kular. It was as if my body already knew what was about to happen because my hands went clammy, and a nasty sickly feeling began to curdle in my stomach.

"Gala?" said Mrs Kular, and at the sound of my name

every pair of eyes in the class turned to stare at me. "Mr Watson would like to see you in his office."

Ross played a *dun-dun-duuuun!* sound on his keyboard. The Eilidhs both gave me curious, concerned looks. I shrugged, trying to seem as if I had no clue what this could be about, then wiped my hands on my trousers and left the classroom. Whispers followed me out, and when I shut the door the draught blew a few words into the corridor. *Wonder.* What. Poems?

Natalie was already waiting outside Mr Watson's office when I got there. She was clutching the straps of her backpack so hard her knuckles had gone white.

"Why are we here?" I whispered. My words came out pale grey and fragile, very different from my usual sturdy font. Natalie shook her head, too stressed to talk, even though there was no one else in the corridor. I rubbed her arm. "It is OK. Maybe it is an error."

After what seemed like hours, the door opened, and Mr Watson appeared. He told us to come into the office and sit down. It had been over two months since I was in here with Papa on my first day. Mr Watson's desk was covered with even more words than there had been back then, so many that you could hardly see the computer keyboard. The headmaster sat down and looked at us with a serious expression.

"Someone 〰〰〰 me that they saw you two 〰〰〰 〰〰〰 words outside the PE department this morning, girls. Is that true?"

I was so panicked that I missed lots of words, but I understood what he was asking.

"No!" I said, frowning. *Who would have told him that?*

"No, we did not."

My voice came out squeaky, and the words were large and red. Mr Watson nodded but his expression didn't change. He swept his arm across the desk to clear a space between the words scattered there.

"Empty your pockets, please, girls. Everything on here."

I quickly stuck my hands in my pockets. There was nothing in there except a hairband, some sweet wrappers and my lunch card, so I put everything on the desk, then folded my arms. Natalie pulled the lining out of her trouser pockets to prove they were empty, then slipped her hands into her jacket. Suddenly her face went white. Mr Watson leaned forward and tapped the desk.

"Everything on the desk, please, Natalie," he said again.

Slowly Natalie opened her hand. Two words,

graceful

and

winter,

fell from her palm to the desk. Mr Watson sat back with a strange look on his face. It wasn't quite a smile but it wasn't a frown, either.

"So were you the only one collecting words, Natalie?" he asked, looking at me. "Or were you both doing this?"

Right then my main feeling was shock – and also anger. Natalie and I had promised each other that we would stop picking up words at school. She must have snuck a few into her pocket when I wasn't around, and now we were both in trouble. Still, I didn't want to lie, and I couldn't let her take the blame for everything.

"No. I have took some too," I said, stammering. "But not today! I stop when you say no more at assembly last week."

Mr Watson didn't look convinced. He opened a drawer and took out a piece of lined paper folded into quarters: the poem that he'd had at assembly on Friday. "Did you send this to Jayne Harris, Natalie? I can give you a pen and paper if you don't feel ~~~~~~ answering."

His words were different when he spoke to her – slower and smooth, but sharp around the edges. Natalie's eyes went wide with panic. I tried to explain that we hadn't sent that poem or the other nasty ones, but nerves made the words clog up my throat. Before I could answer, there was a knock on the door. It swung open, and Ryan stepped into the office.

"I heard you'd asked to see Gala, Mr Watson," he said, his words the smoky colour they always took when he was worried. "Is everything OK?"

While Mr Watson explained why he'd called us here, I wondered again who could have told on us. Natalie might have had words in her pocket but we definitely hadn't gone looking for them this morning – I'd got to school late because I couldn't find my pencil case, so I hadn't even seen her until now. That meant that somebody had lied to get us in trouble.

"Well, Gala told me that she and Natalie *did* make some poems, but not the ones that were ~~~~~~ to Caitlin and the others," Ryan said, looking at me. "You only ~~~~~~ positive ones, to some of their friends. Right, Gala?"

I nodded quickly. Ryan and Mr Watson talked some more, too fast for me to keep up with this time, until the head teacher eventually sighed and turned back to us.

"Well, since there's no ~~~~~~ it was you, you won't be punished for writing the poems." His words were brown, short and pressed tightly together. "But you can both write a letter of ~~~~~~ for taking those words. Hand it in at reception tomorrow morning. And, if I hear about you doing this again, it'll be after-school detention."

The word *apology* fell to the desk and spun towards me. I didn't know what it meant so I looked at Ryan. He explained that we'd have to write a whole page about how sorry we were for picking up the words when Mr Watson said we shouldn't. I could feel a big red shout forming at the back of my throat. I'd been in trouble lots of times back home, usually for talking too much, but not here, and never for something I hadn't done. But I swallowed it down and said OK. Natalie nodded in agreement, and Mr Watson told us to go back to class.

As soon as Ryan shut the door behind us, the anger burst out of me in flame-coloured Catalan. "It's not fair! We haven't done anything wrong!"

Natalie looked like she was about to cry. Ryan patted my back and steered us away from the office.

"I know, girls. I'm sorry. I've been asking the other teachers, trying to find out who might have sent those poems, but no one knows anything." He squeezed my shoulder. "Don't worry. I'll help you with your letter tonight. I'm not much good at writing but I can make us a hot chocolate for inspiration."

That made me give him a reluctant smile. I was glad

I had Ryan here to stand up for us, and I'd never say no to his hot chocolate. But it was still so unfair, and the anger burned in my chest for the rest of the morning.

Gossip travelled fast at our school. By lunchtime, it seemed everyone in first year had heard that Natalie and I had been called into the headmaster's office about the poems. When I walked into Art that afternoon, I found thirty unfriendly faces staring at me.

"Hey, Gala!" Ross put on a fake-friendly voice, his words a sickly yellowish colour. "Got anything else you and Natalie want to get off your chests? Are you going to write a sonnet about me being ginger? Maybe a ~~~~~~ about Rachel's glasses?"

Rachel laughed loudly, and a few others joined in. I opened my mouth to snap back but my words were tangled like spaghetti in my mouth. When I finally managed to speak, they were pale pink and cracked around the edges.

"Natalie and I, we did not write these poems," I stammered, slumping into my seat. "Not the bad ones."

"Well, obviously *you* didn't, Gala," said Rachel, smirking. "You do not speak the English good enough."

There was something weird about the way she was talking. Her voice sounded different, and her words were coming out all misshapen. After a moment, it clicked – she was making fun of my accent. A few people laughed, and a couple copied her. They had never done that before. Not to my face, at least.

My cheeks went bright red, and my eyes started to sting. I knew there was nothing wrong with having a foreign accent – lots of people at home spoke Spanish or Catalan with different accents, like Mariam's mum or the nice Romanian couple who owned the café under our flat. It showed where you came from, and that you had learned another language, and those were both things to be proud of. But I didn't like hearing mine mimicked like that. It made me feel small, alone in this room of people who all sounded the same.

"Gala's English is great," Eilidh O snapped, her words coming out bright red. "You got three out of twenty in French last week, Rachel, so you've got no right to ~~~~~~ someone else's language skills."

"If it's so great, then she knew exactly what she was doing, didn't she?" Caitlin held up the pencil drawing she'd started last week and glowered at me. "You really call this rubbish? It's better than yours."

Tears started to blur my vision. This was so unfair. Natalie and I had only wanted to do something nice, something that would make people feel better. And now we were being blamed and called bullies.

"We did not say that," I said again. The words were even paler now. They fell to the floor without anyone paying them any attention.

"Even the 'nice' poems were weird," Eilidh C muttered, not bothering to look up from the sketch of a guitar that she was working on. "How do you and Natalie know so much about everyone?"

Leonie nodded in agreement. "Yeah, it's like you were ~~~~~~ on us. It's creepy."

Spying. Leonie sat at the desk next to ours, so I spotted the word when it fell on the floor. It took me a moment to work out what it meant. I wanted to tell them that it hadn't been like that. We'd just been paying attention, looking for the things that other people missed. We had written poems for around half the people in this class, Leonie included. Everyone had seemed happy about them at the time, but now a few people nodded. This was all because of those nasty messages. They'd changed everything.

"I believe you."

When I looked around, Eilidh O was smiling at me. The relief was so strong it made a few tears fall down my cheeks. Eilidh O pulled the ends of her sleeves over her hands and used them to pat my face dry.

"Thank you," I sniffed.

"It's OK. And I loved the poem you made for me." Her eyes crinkled as she smiled. "It really did make me feel a bit better about the operation."

Every time someone else gave me a dirty look or muttered something about me under their breath that afternoon, I repeated Eilidh O's words to myself. Natalie and I had made her feel better. We'd done something good. But now that everyone hated us, I wasn't sure it had been worth it.

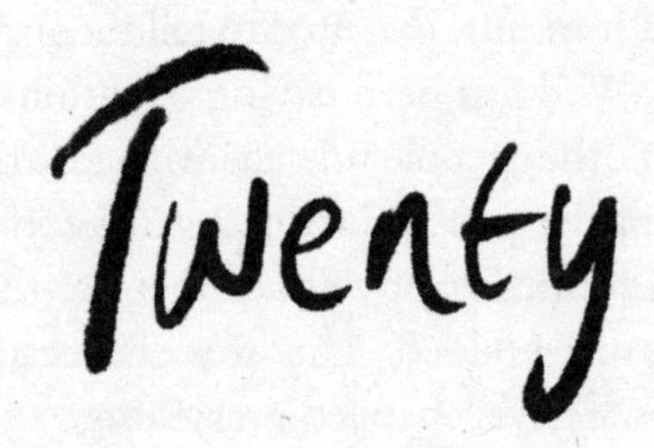

Ryan had rugby coaching after school that day, so I thought I'd have a couple of hours' peace before he came home and Papa found out about what had happened at school. But Ryan must have called him at break or lunchtime because when I stepped into the front room that afternoon Papa greeted me with a big frown on his face.

"What's all this I'm hearing about some poems?" he asked in thundercloud grey. "Ryan told me you were sent to talk to the head teacher about it."

"It was just a misunderstanding, Papa."

Iaia was stretched out on the sofa, watching a show on her tablet, but she turned it off, sat up and patted the seat for me to sit beside her. Dion started licking my face, and Celine climbed up to use me as a cushion, but I didn't even have the energy to laugh. It had been the worst day since I came to Scotland. Maybe my worst day ever.

Papa knelt down to look at me. "Tell me the truth, Gala. Did you write those messages?"

"Gala wouldn't do something like that, Jordi," Iaia said sharply.

"No! It wasn't us!" I said, my words turning from greyish

blue to scarlet in an instant. "Why would we do something like that?"

"You tell me." His voice was calm and steady, but his words were coming out as thin and sharp as icicles. "Did you think that if you got into trouble at school I'd think this was a bad move for us and take you back to Spain?"

There were so many words inside me – angry ones, surprised ones and tons of hurt ones. I sat up and stared at Papa. "Do you *really* think I'd send people horrible messages like that? Do you think I'm a bully?"

"Of course he doesn't, Gala," said Iaia, patting my knee, but Papa didn't answer right away.

My eyes started to water. Ryan had believed me when I said we didn't write the nasty poems. Iaia did too, and Eilidh O. But Papa, the person who was supposed to be on my side, no matter what, thought I was lying.

"I know this has been a hard time for you," he said slowly. "And I know you're still hoping that we'll go back to Cadaqués, but…"

Celine fell back into the sofa cushions with a high-pitched yap as I sat up. "Well, yes, I am," I spat out. "You didn't ask me if I wanted to move here. You and Ryan just decided!"

"I know, Gala. But it's not like I didn't think about how it would affect you." His words had that slightly worn look they always got when he was repeating something for the umpteenth time. "It's a great opportunity for you to experience a new place, learn a new language… It'll open lots of doors."

"I didn't want those doors!" I cried, throwing up my arms. "The only doors I wanted are the ones in our flat.

I want to go home."

"The flat's gone, Gala," Papa snapped. "I got an offer last week. The new owners should be moving in at the end of the month."

The words came out a deep burgundy, and each one hit me like a punch in the stomach. New owners. Strangers in my bedroom, on our balcony, eating dinner in our kitchen. Strangers painting the walls the wrong colours, filling the space with all the wrong things. And Papa had known about it for a *week*.

"Why didn't you tell me before?"

Papa sighed. "I knew how upset you'd be." The words formed a gradient from red to orange, his anger fading more with each one. "I wanted to wait until you were more settled here."

"But the end of the month – that's only a few weeks away. Loads of our stuff is still there!"

"I've arranged to have it put into storage. We'll sort out what we need when we go over at Easter."

So that was it. My plan to move back was ruined. The fact that the flat was still ours was my final hope of ever moving home to Cadaqués, and in a few weeks it would be gone.

"Did you know about this?" I asked Iaia. She bit her lip and looked at me with a sad, guilty expression.

"That's partly why your grandmother's here," Papa said. "There are some forms I had to sign, so she brought them over."

"Jordi!" Iaia reached for my hand. "That's not the reason I came, Gala. I wanted to see you. I could have just posted them otherwise."

That didn't matter – it was another lie. I pulled my hand from her grasp and darted out of the house. I could hear Celine and Dion barking for me to let them out after I'd slammed the door, but for once I didn't want them with me. I ran, my footsteps pounding hard against the path, and kept running until I'd reached the lighthouse at the Point. I opened my lips and shouted so loud the word filled my whole mouth.

"*AAAAAAARGH!*"

I could hear the swish of a golf club nearby, and there were some people walking their dogs further down the beach, but I didn't care who heard. I screamed a second time and a third, then sat down on the sand with a bump. My eyes were stinging but I felt too angry to cry. I stared at the sea, watching the choppy grey waves slip up and down. The dolphins weren't there, of course. They never were. I was starting to wonder if Ryan had made them up.

My head was a tight tangle of thoughts. I had just begun to come to terms with the fact that our move here really was permanent, but it still hurt to know I'd never be in our old home again. That I would never slide across the floral floor tiles in my socks or wiggle the leaky tap in the bathroom to turn it off. That I'd never wake up to the sound of the green birds chattering and cups clinking in the café downstairs.

And the worst part was I hadn't had a chance to say goodbye. If I'd known I was really leaving for good, I would have written my name behind one of the radiators or hidden something under the floorboards. Something to say that I'd been there. That, for a while, that little slice of the world had been mine.

Some time later, I heard footsteps behind me. Iaia and Papa were walking across the sand, Iaia shivering even in her big pink coat. They sat down beside me, and Papa took a bag of barbecue sunflower seeds from his pocket. It was meant as a peace offering but it felt more like a bribe. I pushed the bag away and looked out to sea.

"I'm sorry, bug," Papa said, his words soft and silvery. "I know you'd never bully anyone. I shouldn't have doubted you."

"No, you shouldn't. And you should have told me the flat was gone."

Of everything that had happened, that was perhaps what hurt most: the fact that Ryan and Papa and Iaia had all known about it and kept it from me.

"I know. I was hoping the sale would be finalized after we visited at Easter, but it all happened faster than I expected. I'm sorry." He put his arm round my back. "And I'm sorry that we didn't get to say a proper goodbye to it. I'll miss it too."

I looped my hands round my knees and hid my head in them. "This has been the worst day *ever*. Everything's ruined."

"Nothing's ruined, Gala," Iaia said softly, stroking my hair. "Things will sort themselves out, you'll see."

I didn't look up. I didn't want to feel better yet. I wanted to sulk. But Iaia wasn't the wallowing type, so she got to her feet and tried to pull me up with her. "What would cheer you up? How about a one-woman reggaeton concert?"

"Even better!" Papa jumped up too. "A one-woman-*and*-one-man reggaeton concert."

"Papa, no!"

I shook my head but Iaia was already singing some song that had been a big hit in Spain a few summers ago. Papa grabbed my hands and swung my arms to make me dance. One of the dog walkers was watching, and at first I tried to wriggle out of Papa's grasp, but soon I was laughing so much at his terrible moves that I gave up and joined in. We sang at the top of our voices, littering the sand with big, bright Spanish song lyrics that shone even on this dull grey day. By the time we sat down, we were all out of breath and smiling. My family knew how to get me out of a bad mood like nobody else.

"How about an ice cream?" Papa said, nodding to the van parked up by the lighthouse. "Will that get me out of your bad books?"

I pretended to mull it over. "Maybe if it comes with a stick of chocolate. And caramel sauce. And sprinkles."

As he jogged towards the van, Iaia shuffled along the sand to sit beside me. "Don't take it personally, what he said back at the house," she said quietly. "Jordi's not really himself right now. He's stressed about finding a job, and I think he's more homesick than he wants to admit. He has to make a new life here too, you know. It's not easy for him, either."

I hadn't thought about that. Back home, Papa had tons of friends – they'd always come to the beach with us to play football or volleyball, or we'd go to their houses for dinners that went on so late I'd sometimes fall asleep on the sofa. Here he only had me and Ryan, and we were both at school all day. It must have felt lonely for him sometimes.

"You're probably right." My words were bitter green,

but there were touches of gold around the edges. “I still think I deserve to be in a *bit* of a huff with him, though.”

“Of course you do, chicken! You should have seen the row we had after you left. I haven’t told him off like that since he was fifteen.”

Iaia scowled and wagged her finger, which made me laugh. By the time Papa came back, two ice creams and a cup of coffee balanced in his hands, things between us almost felt back to normal.

Twenty-one

I was wrong when I said that Monday had been the worst day ever. Tuesday was much, much worse.

No one in 1C made any more mean comments about the poems. Instead they all ignored me. Everyone went silent when I walked into registration, then Caitlin and Rachel started giggling in a way that made it very clear they'd been talking about me. Ross pretended he didn't hear me when I asked if I could borrow a pencil in History, and Leonie 'accidentally' knocked my sugar off the worktop in Home Economics. Eilidh O was the only one who was speaking to me, but every time she tried Eilidh C would interrupt and pull her away.

I was on the verge of tears all morning but I knew better than to try and explain we were innocent again. It didn't matter that we hadn't even been punished for writing the poems. As far as everyone in first year was concerned, Natalie and I had been found guilty.

When the bell rang for break, I sprinted down the corridor to find Natalie, but I couldn't see her anywhere. She wasn't at our usual table in the canteen at lunch, and I couldn't find her behind the gym or in the library.

Eventually I asked someone from 1B, and they told me she hadn't come to school today. Part of me was worried about her; another part was just plain mad. First she'd broken Mr Watson's no-wordsearching rule and got us in trouble, and now she'd abandoned me to handle the consequences all by myself.

I knew Eilidh O would have invited me to have lunch with her, Olu and the others, but that wasn't really an option with Eilidh C there. Out of everyone, it especially hurt that she wouldn't believe that I hadn't sent that horrible poem to her. She was supposed to be my friend. How could she think I'd do something like that?

Instead I spent lunchtime in a cubicle in the toilets, looking at my old friends' online profiles. Pau had uploaded a video of himself dunking a basketball. Mariam had posted a photo with her cousin's adorable new kitten. Laia's parents didn't let her have any social-media accounts, but she was in a picture from a school trip to the Dalí museum that another kid in our class had posted, making peace signs outside a bright red building decorated with giant eggs.

The lump in my throat grew bigger and bigger. I missed them all so much. If we hadn't moved away, I'd probably be laughing and playing ping-pong with them right now. Not sitting alone in the toilets, hiding from a bunch of kids who thought I was a bully and a liar.

I kept scrolling, past Christmas and into last year, and soon I started to pop up in the pictures. There was one of us all taken at the theme park that we went to for Pau's birthday. We were zipping down a roller coaster, one so steep that I'd almost chickened out before we reached the entrance, but had forced myself to get on. We all had our eyes shut and screams trailing from our mouths, except for Laia, who was looking at the rest of us and laughing. We hadn't had money to pay for the official photo so Mariam had taken a picture of the display screen on her phone. You could practically hear our voices ringing through the pixels.

Putting down my phone, I stared at my shoes, shiny black against the pale blue bathroom tiles. This hiding-in-the-toilets version of Gala wasn't me. I was the Gala on that roller coaster: brave and fun and **LOUD**. I hadn't felt much like that girl since I came to Scotland, but over the past few weeks I'd started to get her back. There was no way I'd let someone take her away from me now.

So I needed to do something about it.

I got up, washed my hands and headed back to the library. Craig, Abigail and the rest of their group were at the computers, watching Luke playing a shooting game. Before I could lose my nerve, I walked right up to them and tapped Craig on the shoulder. He blinked in surprise when he saw me standing behind him, but then his face stretched into a sneer.

"Look who it is. The *poet*."

His friends turned round and laughed. My cheeks burned but I tightened my fists and took a deep breath.

"I need to speak with you." I had made a note of what I wanted to say on my phone as I walked to the library, and my words came out firm and mahogany-coloured, a lot like Papa's when he'd made his mind up about something. "Now."

"*Okaaay*," Craig said. "What about?"

"Not here. Outside."

Abigail made an annoying 'oooh' noise. Craig shot her a dirty look, but either curiosity or the determination in my words made him push his chair back and follow me. I led him through the side door and out to the steps at the back of the school. The football team were practising on the pitch across the road, but there was no one else around.

I came right out with it. "Did you write the poems? The bad ones? To Abigail and the others?"

Craig blinked again, then let out a short laugh. "What? No. Those are ~~~~~~."

Pathetic. His words came out in bold brownish-red letters. They looked and sounded like the truth but I swallowed and pushed on.

"I do not believe you. I think it was you," I said, though really I had no idea. I just needed to ask someone. Do something to make this stop. And if Craig hadn't written them he might have an idea who had. Who better to understand a bully than a bully?

"Why would I do that?" Craig frowned and gestured towards the library. "Abigail got one of those. She's my mate. I don't say that kind of ~~~~~~ to my friends. Well, OK, I do but it's just banter."

"Because –" I fumbled around, putting the sentence together in my head – "we send you a poem, a good one, and you do not say anything."

Craig's cheeks flushed. "Yeah, because it was ~~~~~~ weird! It was like you were … I don't know, like you were trying to get into my head or something. Like you wanted to ~~~~~~ me like the child psychiatrist."

His words had turned bright red now, and they were

coming out too fast for me to catch them all. But I could tell from the anger and indignation in them that they were honest.

"It is really not you?" I asked.

"No! The first poems were weird, but those other ones were stupid."

I put my hands on my hips. "So who was it?"

He shrugged. "How am I supposed to know?"

My resolve came seeping out of me like a flat tyre. I sat down on the step with a bump. If Craig hadn't written the poems, and he didn't know who had, I was out of ideas. Abigail would have been my next suspect, but why would she write nasty things about herself? It didn't make any sense.

"Did you and Natalie not do it either then?" Craig said after a moment.

"No! I have said this many, many times, but they think we are liars."

My words came out all wobbly. I crushed them under my foot and left a watery lilac smudge on the ground.

"No one believes me."

Craig was quiet for a moment. I kept my eyes on the ground, waiting to hear footsteps and the door slamming behind him. But he didn't leave. Instead he sat down on the step beside me, keeping a wide gap between us.

"I know what that's like. Teachers are always blaming me for stuff. My mum and dad too. They don't even 〰〰 asking me what's happened half the time. If

something

goes wrong,

they think

it must be

my fault."

His words fell on to the step where I was sitting. They were dark red but blue around the edges. I knew what he was talking about because I'd seen it happen. Teachers would hear someone sniggering while they were writing on the board and say, "Quiet, Craig," without even looking to see if he was the one mucking around. A lot of the time it was him but sometimes he was getting on with his work, and he got the blame anyway.

"Well, I am sorry that I did this too. That I … was blaming you," I said, seeing the word he'd used on the stone step, "without to ask you first."

Craig stared at me. Something about my apology had caught him off guard. For a long moment he didn't seem to know what to say.

"Yeah, well, sorry for the stuff I said about Natalie," he said, looking towards the football pitch. "I didn't mean most of it. It's just to get a laugh."

"For her it is not funny," I said, my words a sharp orange now. "So stop it, please."

"All right, I'll try." Craig linked his hands behind his head and sighed. "Sometimes stuff comes out of my mouth without me thinking."

"So, think more."

"OK, OK, I will." He looked at me for another few seconds, then let out a short laugh. "I didn't realize you were this…"

"This what?"

"Nothing. You're just different from what I thought."

He pushed himself to his feet but paused before he opened the side door. I turned round to see what he was waiting for. When he looked down at me, there was a spark of something in his eye.

"You and Natalie – you were collecting those words for a while, right? See, whoever else is writing the poems probably didn't." His words were a bright green colour that I'd never seen from him before. "They probably needed to make loads by themselves, so their own words will be on those poems too."

I thought about it. "You're right. I will speak with Natalie about it. Thank you."

He almost smiled, but then he shrugged, and the old Craig was back, the one who took nothing seriously. "Or whatever. I don't care." He pulled the door open. "But good luck, I guess."

Twenty-two

Three lonely classes and two more mean comments in the corridors later, I was exhausted and desperate to go home. Ryan was taking rugby practice, and Papa had gone to another job interview, but Iaia and the dogs were waiting for me in the kitchen when I got in. As soon as I saw Iaia's smiling face, I burst into tears.

"Everyone hates me," I sobbed as she rushed forward to give me a hug. "And Natalie's disappeared, and I don't know who wrote those stupid poems, and I keep saying it wasn't us, but no one's listening. I wish we'd never come here."

My words were deep purple and blurry around the edges. Iaia brushed a few from my collar and kissed the top of my head.

"No one hates you, chicken." She put her hands on my cheeks while Dion nuzzled his head against my arm and whimpered softly. "I'm going to make you something to eat, and then we'll take the dogs out. A walk will do you good."

Iaia set about making me a sandwich while I went upstairs to get changed out of my uniform and wash my face.

I felt a little better once I'd eaten and Celine had let me pet her but I didn't really want to go for a walk – there was too much chance we'd bump into someone from school. I couldn't handle any more dirty looks or accusations.

"Nobody's going to say anything to you with this guy around." Iaia petted Dion's giant head, then spun round and did a high kick into a karate pose. "Or me!"

I laughed reluctantly and went to put my shoes on. As I was tying the laces, the doorbell rang. Iaia had gone to the bathroom so I went to answer it, expecting the postman. Instead Natalie was standing on our front step.

"I'm sorry." She spoke the words into her palm and pressed them into my hand. They were a dozen mottled shades of blue. "I should have told you I wasn't coming to school today. How did it go?"

I pointed to my eyes, still red from crying. "How you think?"

Natalie winced. "I'm really sorry, Gala. I should have come with you. I just couldn't face that place today. Or Mr Watson or Craig or … any of them."

"It's OK." I poked at the edges of her apology with my finger. I could feel the guilt and sadness in the words. She really meant what she was saying. "But one question. Yesterday did you pick up the two words that Mr Watson shows us?"

"No, I definitely didn't! Those must have been in there for a few days. I guess I missed them when I ~~~~~~ my pockets." Some of the anger I'd been feeling towards her slipped away when I saw how upset she looked. "Whoever told Mr Watson they saw me do it was lying. I think they're trying to frame us."

"Frame?" I repeated. I knew what a picture frame was, but that didn't make sense here.

"Make us look guilty," said Natalie. "Get us in trouble."

"Oh." Celine was sniffing at Natalie's shoes, so I picked her up and let her wriggle around in my arms. "Well, it is not Craig. I spoke with him this afternoon."

"You did?" She blinked. "Wow. What did he say?"

I told her everything that Craig had said, including the part about how we might be able to work out who sent the poems by finding their own words in them. Natalie's eyebrows rose.

"That's actually a good idea," she said. "But how are we going to do that if we don't have the pieces of paper?"

Before I could answer, Iaia came out of the bathroom and into the hallway. Her face broke into a big smile when she saw we had a visitor. "Oh, hello! Is this the famous Natalie?"

I'd already told Iaia that Natalie got anxious around new people, so she didn't swoop in to kiss each cheek like she would with my friends back home. Instead she asked Natalie if she wanted to come for a walk with us, warm yellow and orange words that Natalie couldn't understand falling round her feet. When I explained what Iaia had said, Natalie took out her phone and asked me if I'd be OK with her tagging along.

"Yes, come," I said, even though I was still a bit mad at her. We needed to work out what to do next.

The dogs went bounding ahead of us, barking happily. We ended up walking to the Fairy Glen, the place that Natalie had mentioned the very first time we had lunch together. I'd never been there before but I could instantly see why she liked it so much. It was a quiet woodland walkway along a small, babbling river. Countless birds twittered and flitted between the branches overhead, and the ground was carpeted with snowdrops and daffodils.

"It's like something from a fairy tale!" Iaia said.

Even though it was new to me too, I felt a tiny bump of pride that I got to be the one to show it to her.

After a while, we came to a clearing with a small waterfall spilling into a rock pool. Natalie had already told me about this spot – she came here by herself sometimes, to think or to go wordsearching. The dogs were busy exploring, and Iaia was taking photos to send to her friends, so Natalie and I sat on a big rock by the water. While I picked at the grapes and biscuits Iaia had brought, Natalie wrote me a message on her phone.

I think the person who lied to Mr Watson about seeing us collecting words is almost definitely the same person leaving the bad poems. They obviously knew that we're wordsearchers, so I think they probably worked out we were the ones writing the good poems some time ago. They sent the nasty poems to get us into trouble – and it worked.

"But why do they want to get us in trouble?" I asked once I'd read the whole note. There were people who didn't like Natalie just because she was different. There were probably others who didn't like me for the same reason. But to go this far to make life difficult for us…? That was quite scary.

"What are you girls talking about?" Iaia asked, climbing on to the rock beside us.

Iaia already knew most of the story about the words and the poems, so I filled her in on Natalie's theory. She listened as she nibbled on a biscuit, her thin eyebrows knitted in a frown.

"Do you think your headmaster still has the poems? They might have been given to him as evidence."

I shook my head – I'd seen Eilidh and Caitlin crumple their poems up, and Ben's and Abigail's had both been ripped in two. But, when I told Natalie what Iaia had said, she grabbed my arm.

"He did have one when we were in his office, remember? The one sent to Jayne. Maybe it's still there!"

Her words came out quiet and the colour of milky tea. It took me a moment to realize that she was talking in front of Iaia and how unusual that was for Natalie, but she seemed a lot calmer than at school. Iaia had that effect on people. She dressed all kooky and colourful, but she had that cosy gran vibe too. She felt safe.

When I translated Natalie's reply, Iaia nodded. "There you go then. You can ask him if he still has it. Or talk to Ryan. He could go and fetch it for you."

I shook my head quickly. I didn't want to go back to Mr Watson – we might make things even worse for ourselves – and Papa would be annoyed if I asked Ryan to get involved. I explained all of this to Iaia in Catalan. Natalie read my words as they fell on to my lap. She picked up a purple **oficina**.

"Mr Watson always locks his office when he leaves it," she said, touching the edges of the word. "Some fourth-year kids snuck in there during assembly and stole his cactus a few years ago, so now he never leaves it open.

But they keep the spare set of keys at reception."

"How do you know this?" I asked.

She grinned at me. "I notice things."

Iaia was giving me a quizzical look now, so I quickly explained what Natalie had said. Translating from English to Catalan and back again was making my head spin, but I was enjoying it too. It felt good to be the one connecting two people who didn't share the same language. Not that they needed it to get along – right now Natalie was laughing as Iaia imitated Celine, who was snapping at her ankles, demanding a piece of biscuit.

"You think..." The idea seemed ridiculous, but I said it anyway. "You think maybe we can take the keys and enter the office?"

Natalie nodded slowly. "We'll be in so much trouble if we get caught, but how else are we going to prove it wasn't us?"

"Uh-oh." Iaia grinned. "I can understand mischief in any language. What are you two plotting?"

I thought about making something up but Iaia always knew when I was lying. I reluctantly repeated what I'd said, waiting for her to tell us that we shouldn't go snooping around, that we'd get into even more trouble, that she was going to tell Papa – all the things grown-ups usually say when you want to do something risky. Instead my grandmother popped a grape into her mouth and waggled her eyebrows.

"Maybe I can help."

Twenty-three

We called it the Big Plan, and we decided it would happen during assembly on Friday. It was the perfect time: Mr Watson's office would be empty, and all the other teachers would be in the main hall, so there'd be no one to catch us sneaking around. We just needed a good excuse so they'd let us leave early.

"I'll pretend to be sick," Natalie said while we were plotting outside the PE department at lunchtime. "You can say I need you to explain to the school nurse what's wrong, and that way you can come with me."

The sickbay was right beside reception and down the corridor from Mr Watson's office, so if we were really, really quick we could grab the keys, unlock the door and find the poem in under a few minutes. It was a dangerous plan but the best – and only – one we had. We had to give it a shot.

On Friday morning, I went to assembly with a fluttering heart and trembling hands. It had been four days since Mr Watson hauled us into his office, and despite what Papa and Ryan kept saying the kids in our class weren't showing any signs of forgiving or forgetting about the poems. As we sat down in the front row, someone flicked a word towards us, and it got caught in Natalie's hair.

Liar. Thin strokes, rust-coloured.

I picked it out and squashed it under the heel of my shoe. We'd prove them wrong. We had to.

Mr Watson started the assembly by recapping what had gone on in the week, then went on to talk about the sports day that was coming up. As usual, I zoned out pretty quickly. My stomach felt funny from all the nerves, and my right knee kept jigging up and down. The word *liar* shone like a neon sign on the back of my eyelids.

Suddenly there was a big thump beside me. When I looked round, Natalie was lying on the ground, her eyes closed and her mouth open. A few people around us gasped and got to their feet. Mr Watson was cut off mid-sentence, slate-grey words dangling from his lower lip. I was so shocked that I forgot all about our plan and knelt to check Natalie was still breathing.

"Natalie? Are you OK?"

Everyone in the hall was staring at us. When Natalie had said she was going to pretend to be sick, I thought she'd put up her hand and let a teacher know she had a sore head or a bad stomach. Not that she was going to keel over like a felled tree. Ryan came running across the hall with Miss Shah right behind him.

"Natalie?" Miss Shah said, patting Natalie's chalky cheek. "I think she's fainted."

Slowly Natalie's eyelids fluttered open. Ryan and I helped her sit up and another teacher came over with a bottle of water. They all looked so worried that for a moment I felt bad that this was all pretend. Natalie took a sip of water, gave a wobbly smile and made the OK sign to show she was fine.

"Go and have a lie-down in the sickbay," Miss Shah said. "Are you able to walk there?"

"You go with her, Gala." Ryan helped Natalie to her feet and steered her towards me. "Tell Mr Nowak that she's not feeling well."

Hundreds of pairs of eyes followed us as we made our way through the hall, my arm round Natalie's back and hers round my shoulder like she might collapse again at any moment. It was almost funny – people barely seemed to notice Natalie or me before this week, and since Monday we'd been sent to the head teacher's office *and* caused a scene at Friday assembly.

"You should be an actor," I whispered once we were in the empty corridor. "That was astounding."

She gave me a weak grin and leaned her weight against me, committed to her role as Fainting Girl #1. When we got to the entrance of the school, there was a woman with short grey hair in a bright pink coat talking to the receptionist. My stomach did another somersault with nerves. This was Stage Two of our plan – where Iaia came in.

"Here," she was saying in English, like we had rehearsed. "This place."

She was pointing to a map of Fortrose that we had printed out at Ryan's. Natalie had even borrowed her stepdad's old camera to make Iaia look like an authentic tourist. The receptionist, Miss Reeves, was smiling, but she looked confused. I had to press my lips together really hard to stop myself from laughing as we walked past and knocked on the door of the sickbay. When Mr Nowak answered, I explained what had happened.

"Did you have breakfast this morning?" he asked Natalie. She shook her head and he smiled. "Probably low blood sugar then. Have a lie-down. You can stay if you like," he added to me. "Just until assembly is over."

He gestured to the small bed in the corner and went back to the storage cupboard at the back of the sickbay. Natalie and I looked at each other. She swallowed and then made a fist to say *you can do it*. Iaia probably couldn't keep Miss Reeves busy for much longer. If we were really going to do this, it had to be now.

"No, it is OK," I said loudly enough for Mr Novak to hear. "I will go back to assembly."

My nerves were so bad I thought I might actually throw up, but I turned and hurried out of the room. Luckily Miss Reeves had left the desk and was now standing at the door with Iaia and pointing towards the high street, exactly as we'd planned. Moving as quietly as I could, I snuck behind the desk and looked for the keys. They were right where Natalie had told me they'd be, on a little hook behind the computer. I grabbed them and ran as quickly as I could towards Mr Watson's office.

That was when I realized I had no idea which of the dozen or so keys opened the door. I tried one at random, but it didn't fit. Neither did the second, or the third. Hands shaking, I slid another key in and turned. This one moved! I pushed down on the door handle and…

"Gala? What are you doing?"

All the blood drained from my face at the sound of a very

familiar voice. Ryan was standing at the end of the corridor, a look of total shock on his face. I was so startled, I forgot he was Mr Young at school and asked in an affronted voice, "What are *you* doing?"

"I came to see how Natalie was feeling," he said. "Are – are those the ∿∿∿∿∿ keys to the office? Where did you get those?"

"In reception. We need to find the bad poems."

I started explaining in English but the words got all tangled up with my nerves, and I switched to Catalan. Ryan's eyes zigzagged left to right as he tried to read along, but from the way he sighed I could tell he understood what I needed. He looked over his shoulder again, then pushed open the door.

"You wait here. I'll take a look."

He went into the office and hurried over to Mr Watson's desk. He leafed through the papers piled there, checked the drawers and the waste-paper basket, then shook his head. My heart sank. Of course it wasn't here. It had been four days since we were in the office – the head teacher had probably thrown it away, and no doubt the cleaning staff emptied the bins every day. It suddenly seemed so silly that we'd thought otherwise.

"It's not here, Gala." Ryan locked the door again and put the keys in his pocket. "You really, really shouldn't have done that. You'd have been in huge trouble if anyone else had caught you."

He pressed the words into the dark carpet with the toe of his shoe so no one would see them later. They were dark pink and smaller than usual, the letters crammed together tight instead of his usual loopy font. He was annoyed.

I don't think I'd ever seen Ryan this annoyed before.

"Sorry," I said, small and blue. "Will you tell Papa?"

"I don't know." Ryan ran a hand through his hair and sighed. "Probably not. Jordi's stressed enough as it is without worrying about you ~~~~~~ and entering. But I am giving you detention for Monday. You and Natalie."

My mouth fell open. "Seriously?"

"Yes, seriously." The shape of his words was so sharp, so unlike Ryan, that it made me take a step back. "Assembly's just about over. Get Natalie and go to your class."

I wanted to apologize again but he turned round, left the keys at reception and headed to the PE department without looking back. The nerves in my stomach curled into nausea. If Ryan was this mad, we really must have crossed a line.

When I got back to the sickbay, Natalie was lying down with her eyes closed and one hand clamped over her forehead. Hearing me come in, she sat up and swung her legs over the side of the bed. There was an excited expression on her face, but I shook my head.

"It was not there. And Ryan has seen me, so we both have detention on Monday."

To my surprise, Natalie grinned and reached into her schoolbag. She brought out a scrap of paper ripped roughly into the shape of a triangle. When she passed it to me, my heart leaped: there were two lines of spoken words stuck to the page.

"You finded it!" I remembered as soon as I said it that it was 'found', not 'finded', but in that moment I was too happy to care. "Where?"

She pointed towards reception, picked up her bag and jacket and left the room. Following her out, I noticed that there was a paper recycling bin behind Miss Reeves's seat. All that effort snatching the keys and sneaking into the office and the clue we needed had been at reception all along. I didn't know whether to laugh or cry! I looked down at the paper and studied the part of the poem that was visible.

Jayne, *Jayne*, **go** away,

You're **so** *annoying* every day.

Jayne –

"Oh wow, so clever and nice," I said – I'd noticed that I was more sarcastic in English than I was in my other languages.

Natalie pointed to ***Jayne***'s name and the word ***annoying***. They were both the same purplish red and both made of up delicate letters that sloped to the right, as if they'd been whispered. There was no doubt they'd come from the same person. Now we needed to find who they belonged to.

People were starting to move into the hallway so assembly must have ended. I turned towards our next class but Natalie grabbed my sleeve and pointed to the front door. Iaia was standing at the end of the road, still pretending to look at her map. I glanced around to check no teachers were about, then slipped outside to meet her.

"Iaia! Thank you!" I ran towards her and threw my arms

round her in a big hug. "You were awesome."

"Glad I could help, chicken. Just don't tell your papa, or I won't be allowed back to visit." She gave me a big grin. "Did you find the poem?"

I felt a big kick of guilt as I remembered Ryan's angry expression. "Yes, but not in the office. Natalie found a piece in the recycling bin."

"Oh, smart girl. I spotted her rummaging around in there while that nice receptionist was trying to give me directions." Iaia jabbed the map with her finger. "I almost feel like I should go and see this little museum after she spent so long telling me how to get there, but I need to start packing."

Iaia's flight back to Spain was booked for the next morning. The thought of it made my heart twist. It had only been a week but I'd got used to her singing in the kitchen and cackling at the TV shows she watched on her tablet. The house felt fuller with her in it.

"I don't want you to go," I said, making my words long and high-pitched and forget-me-not blue. "Can I come back with you?"

"We'd have to take Celine and Dion, and I don't think we can fit you all in my suitcase." Iaia laughed and pointed back to the school. "Anyway, you'd better get back in there. You and Natalie have a criminal to find!"

Twenty-four

Papa, Ryan and I took Iaia to Inverness to catch her flight home the next morning. It was a small airport, but surprisingly busy – there were so many words strewn across the floor, I could hardly see my shoes. I nudged at them with my feet while Iaia went up to the desk to check in her suitcase. There were some interesting ones – a sparkling silver *miss*, a cherry-red **minutes** that had obviously been said by someone in a panic, and quite a lot in other languages – but, with everything going on at school, collecting words had lost some of its shine for me.

I left them behind and followed everyone to the security gates. When Iaia held out her arms to me, I burst into tears for the second time that week.

"Don't cry, chicken! I'm going to see you in a few weeks!" she said, wrapping me up in a big hug.

"That's too long." I pressed my face into Iaia's pink coat. "Can't you stay a bit longer?"

"I've got to get back, Galeta. My padel tournament is next Saturday, remember? I can't let Pilar snatch the trophy again. She'd be insufferable." She laughed and kissed my head. When I moved away, my tears left wet smudges on

Hurry on faim puerta durstig delay morgen obrigado abfahrt familia gate her coat. "Only three weeks. You'll be there before you know it."

After that, Iaia hugged Papa and Ryan, then me again, and then she walked through the security gates, and we couldn't see her any more. Three weeks. Grown-ups were always saying time would fly by, but a week could feel like forever. Three was like a triple eternity. And, in my case, it was a triple eternity of being one of the most unpopular girls in first year.

The car felt too quiet without Iaia on the way home. Ryan suggested we go out for lunch, and, when neither Papa nor I had any suggestions, took us to a little village by the sea. A row of cafés and restaurants was perched above a pebble beach, and outside one of them was a single palm tree. It was tall and lopsided, and some of its fronds were falling off from the strong winds we'd had recently, but it was such an obvious reminder of home that I started crying again.

Papa put his arm round my shoulders. "I know it's tough, bug. I miss her a lot too. But we'll see her again really soon."

He tried to pull me in for a hug but I wriggled away from him and walked down the steps and on to the beach. Papa called after me but Ryan told him to give me some space. He'd kept his word about not telling Papa about the Big Plan, and by the time he got home from school yesterday he'd been back to his usual smiley self. But that detention hovered between us, an uncomfortable secret.

I walked along the beach for fifteen minutes, stopping every so often to skim stones across the water. Sometimes

I would say a word out loud and stretch it round the pebble before I threw it in. *Homesick*. Three bounces and into the water. *Lonely*. Four bounces and gone. *School*. Five bounces, then down to the bottom of the ocean.

Soon I'd stopped feeling like I was going to cry, and I was starting to get hungry, so I headed back to Papa and Ryan. They were sitting at a table outside one of the restaurants with coffee cups and sandwiches in front of them. Before I walked up the stairs to join them, something in Papa's tone caught my attention.

"I thought she was settling in so well." He was talking in Catalan, which surprised me because he always spoke to Ryan in English. "But she's been so sad lately, and now she's getting into trouble… I've never seen her like this before."

"This stuff at school's getting to her," Ryan said in English. "I've spoken to her form teacher about it but she just keeps saying it'll pass."

"Well, it will. You know how kids are. They'll forget all this in a few days."

Ryan was quiet for a moment. "I don't know, Jordi. I know everyone says kids are so ~~~~~~, but we've put her through such a big change. Maybe it wasn't a good idea, bringing her over here."

"But we are a family," Papa said, switching to English now. "I want us to be together. All three of us."

"Of course we're a family, babe. That's not going to change. But maybe… Maybe we need to rethink things."

Another long silence. "What are you saying?"

"I don't know." Ryan sighed. "Maybe we should go back to the way things were before. Visiting each other once a month or so."

"No. No," Papa said, and now I could hear the panicked red colour of his words, even if I couldn't see them. "That was exhausting. It wasn't good for either of us, or for her. Anyway, I just sold the apartment!"

"I know, but you could stay with your mum. You could rent somewhere. I don't want Gala to be miserable." Ryan took a sip of his coffee. When he spoke again, his words were thick. "I mean… I'm sort of her parent too, right? So that means putting her first."

They slipped into silence, and I slid down the wall. If I had overheard this conversation a couple of months ago, I'd already be packing my bags and phoning my friends to tell them I was coming home. This was all I'd wanted. And, in a way, it was the solution to my problems – when I was back at my old school in Cadaqués, I wouldn't care if a bunch of kids in another country thousands of kilometres away still hated me for something I hadn't done.

But instead their words left a strange, hollow feeling in my stomach. I pictured Papa and me back in our old life but now it felt wrong without Ryan there. I'd miss our walks home from school or to the Point with the dogs. I'd miss how he'd make me hot chocolate or play games with me when Papa was busy, the trails of shiny song lyrics he left across the carpet every morning. I thought about him saying that he was sort of my parent too, and I realized it was true. He'd believed me about the poems and stuck up for me in front of Mr Watson. He'd snuck into the headmaster's office to search for evidence, even though it could have got him in trouble. Wherever we ended up living, it would feel empty without Ryan.

Like the last few flakes of a shaken snow globe, my mixed-up feelings about Fortrose and Cadaqués finally fell into place. I missed Iaia. I missed my friends, and I probably always would. But things had changed now. And if going back to Spain meant leaving Ryan behind – leaving part of our family behind – then I didn't want it. Not any more.

I ran up the steps so quickly, Papa and Ryan both jumped. I put on a big smile and made my words sunshine yellow. "Hi! I feel better now. Can I have a sandwich?"

"Oh. Of course, bug." Papa blinked and pushed one of the bags towards me as I sat down. "I got you ham and cheese, or there's tuna mayonnaise, or…"

"Ham and cheese is good."

I didn't mention their conversation – I didn't want them to know I'd been eavesdropping. Instead I launched into this so-bad-it-was-good joke that Frankie had told me a few weeks before, talking so fast some of the words got stuck to the top of my mouth. Ryan and Papa both laughed, and then Ryan shared an even worse joke one of the fourth years had told him, and the fake smile I'd plastered on slipped into something real. Maybe it was just the sandwich but I actually *did* feel a little better.

Even so, I didn't want to carry on at school if I was going to be a social pariah for the next five years. Natalie and I had that scrap of poem, our one piece of evidence. Now we had to clear our names.

Twenty-five

When the bell rang after our last class on Monday, Natalie and I both went upstairs to the Business classroom for the detention that Ryan had given us. There were seven other kids in there, including Eilidh C, all sitting at desks while Mr Rossi marked homework. I took the desk to Eilidh's right.

"You are here too?" I whispered.

"Got in trouble for talking too much." She rolled her eyes. "Second time this month."

That surprised me. Eilidh C left mountains of words behind her wherever she went, but she was also a bit of a suck-up, and she usually managed to talk her way out of trouble with the teachers. She must have really been overdoing it to get detention twice in a month.

"It'll be a third if you don't get on with your work, Eilidh," Mr Rossi said, glancing up from his marking.

"Yes, sir," Eilidh said, her words a bored grey. When Mr Rossi looked down, she pulled a face.

I chuckled quietly but she didn't grin at me like she might have done a few weeks ago. Things hadn't been the same between us since the bad poems, even if she wasn't ignoring me any more. Eilidh O had tried to talk to her about it but Eilidh C still didn't believe that Natalie and I were innocent. It was yet another reason I wanted to find out who was behind this.

Natalie had already started on her French homework, so I took out the list of idioms that Miss Shah had given me in my English class. When the bell rang forty-five minutes later, I'd memorized ten expressions related to food. My favourites were *to use your noodle* and *cool as a cucumber*, and I was already planning on trying them out on Papa and Ryan when I got home.

Eilidh C raced out of the room without saying goodbye. I waited for Natalie to pack up her stuff and followed her out of the classroom. Suddenly Natalie grabbed my arm so tight, I actually shouted out. With her other hand, she pointed to a spot on the floor. The entire corridor was flooded with words, so it took me a moment to see what Natalie was seeing: a small ***unfair***, shining like a spot of red wine in the overhead lights. I knelt to take a closer look.

"That is it!" We'd been searching since Friday for a word like the one in Jayne's poem. This was the exact same colour, the same-shaped letters. "Maybe there is more."

Natalie pointed for me to go left while she looked to the right. Finding what we were looking for among a whole day's worth of speech was like doing one of the wordsearch puzzles that Miss Shah sometimes gave me, only a *hundred* times harder. It took almost five minutes but eventually I found another word in the same colour and shape: ***this***.

"I have it!" I called to Natalie. Her eyes brightened, and she waded through the words to join me at the end of the corridor. A few minutes later, she spotted another word, ***believe***, and then I saw a tiny ***sake*** clinging to the bannister at the top of the stairs. I picked them up, followed the trail downstairs and towards the Music room, where there was a red ***again*** stuck to the door. Voices were coming from inside. Natalie and I looked at each other. Her hand curled round the door handle. My heart began to pound.

"Do it," I whispered.

In one swift motion, Natalie pulled the door open. Inside, two cleaners were busy sweeping the words into the giant blue bins that they used to collect them. They both jumped when they heard us come in.

"You scared us there, girls!" one woman said, pressing her hand to her chest. "Have you lost something?"

"No, nothing," I said, my shoulders slumping in time with Natalie's. "Sorry."

When we turned round, my heart sank even further. Mr Watson was standing in the corridor, his coat on and his bag slung over his shoulder, watching us. He frowned and took a step forward.

"What are you two still doing here?" he asked but my mind had gone blank and I couldn't find the words to reply. When we didn't answer, he pointed to me. "What have you got there, Gala?"

A big Spanish swear word appeared on the back of my tongue. I swallowed it down and held out my hand. On my palm were the culprit's words: ***this***, ***believe***, ***sake***, ***again***, shimmering in purplish red. Mr Watson's eyes narrowed.

"I'm disappointed, Gala. You know that's not allowed." He sighed, though there didn't seem to be any disappointment in his thick brassy words. He pulled a pad of white slips from his pocket. "I'm giving you three more days of detention. Both of you."

"But, sir…" I started to protest, but the words still wouldn't come. As Mr Watson scribbled down our names, it was clear he wasn't listening anyway.

By the time Natalie and I got out of school, it was almost five o'clock. I was in a really bad mood after what had happened with Mr Watson but I cheered up a bit when Natalie asked if I wanted to come to hers for tea. I texted Papa to ask if that was OK. As far as he knew, I'd stayed at school late to do my homework with Natalie – which was mostly true. Papa replied with a gif of SpongeBob giving a thumbs up, and minutes later Natalie and I arrived at the little white cottage.

Inside, Natalie's mum was making dinner while her stepdad, Charlie, did the ironing, and Ava watched cartoons.

"Here's my rebel." Abby waved a wooden spoon at us when she saw us come in, her words the colour of cinnamon. "How was detention, James Dean?"

I didn't know who that was but Natalie grinned. "Quite useful actually. I got a lot of homework done. And…" She whipped the detention slip out of her pocket and put it on the table with a flourish. "We just got three more days of it."

"Three days?" Charlie echoed. He was a small, thin man with a shaved head and glasses. They steamed over as he pressed the iron into one of Natalie's school jumpers.

"Steady on, Nat. What have you done this time?"

Natalie explained what had happened. She'd told me her parents had been not-so-secretly delighted that she'd been given her first-ever detention – they saw it as a sign she was 'coming out of her shell' – but now they looked worried. Ava interrupted by shouting a bright yellow, "Hello!" and sliding down from the table to come and see us. She was holding a spatula and presented it to me like it was an important gift.

"Thank you very much," I said seriously.

Natalie picked Ava up and swung her round. Ava screeched, clapped her hands, then demanded to be put down so she could press the buttons on the washing machine.

"Let's go up to my room," Natalie said to me.

"Be back down for tea in twenty minutes," Abby said. "We need to have a conversation about this detention ~~~~~~, OK?"

"Yes, Mother." Natalie's words came out in silly voice and a cartoonish font, like she was joking, but when we got to her bedroom she fell face first on to her bed and let out a long, loud groan.

"Are you OK?" I asked.

"Yeah. Sorry." She rolled over and clutched her hair in her hands. "I'm annoyed that we didn't find where those words came from. I doubt we'll ever work out who it was now."

I lay down on the bed beside her. There were glow-in-the-dark stars stuck to her ceiling. I had the exact same ones in my room in Cadaqués. Thinking about them, I realized I didn't take them off before we left. I wondered really

if they were still there or whether the new owners had picked them off already.

real

"This sucks," Natalie said. She said the word *sucks* with such force, it flew upwards, then landed back on her nose. I giggled.

suck

"It *really* sucks." I put the stress on the *really*, then quickly blew to keep it up in the air. It hovered above me for a few seconds before landing on my forehead.

"At least I have you," Natalie said. "Even with all this going on, school has been so much better since you got here."

"I agree," I said, putting my hand on my heart. "I am … so amazing."

Natalie rolled her eyes and pushed my face away, and I laughed. It was good to know that, no matter how bad things got, I'd have her on my side. But I missed hanging around with the Eilidhs, Olu, Frankie and the others too. I'd always liked being part of a group, and I wanted other friends as well as Natalie. I wanted people to see how great she was too. Or, at the very least, I wanted people not to hate us.

"Maybe we do this wrong." I propped myself up against her giant doughnut pillow. "We have said again and again that we do not write the bad poems. But maybe we need to say that we *do* write the good poems."

Natalie looked up at me. "How will that help?"

"We explain why we are wordsearchers," I said. "Why it is important for us. Then they will see that we would not do something bad with the words we find."

"I don't think they'll get it," Natalie said. "People will understand why talking in English is hard for you, sure.

But not even Charlie fully understands selective mutism. When he first met my mum, he kept trying to push me into speaking. He thought I was being shy or sulky. He's much better now – he even started learning sign language to communicate with me when I was younger. It took him a while to get there, though."

"Maybe you are right," I said. "But maybe one person or two will listen and understand. It is better than nothing, no?"

Natalie was quiet for a long moment. I waited for her to put her words together, my eyes fixed on the plastic stars. Maybe I should ask Papa to get some for my new bedroom. I liked looking up at them at night, and they'd go nicely with my galaxy lamp.

"How would we even try to explain?" Natalie asked eventually. She picked up the light green *listen* that had fallen from my mouth and turned it in her fingers. "I don't think more poems is a good idea."

"Maybe a letter? Or a story?"

"Yeah, maybe. A story might be nice. We could write one with words from our collections." Natalie's eyes brightened at the idea. "Who cares if Mr Watson finds out? All he's going to do is give us yet more detentions."

I grinned and nodded. We'd both missed wordsearching and creating things from our collections, and detention really wasn't so bad. Like Natalie said, it meant we got our homework done before leaving school, and that way we had the rest of the evening free. But, if we were going to write a story, that left us with the question of how we were going to tell it.

"We could take a photo or make a video," said Natalie.

"We'd just need to upload it and email the link to everyone in our year."

That didn't feel personal enough. Each of the words we'd collected was filled with feelings. We couldn't get that across in an image.

"Assembly," I said. "We can do it in Friday assembly."

Natalie pushed herself up on one elbow and stared at me. "You know you'd have to do the talking… Do you really want to do that in front of the whole school?"

A few months ago, the thought of having to speak in English for that long and with that many people watching would have terrified me. It still did, really, but not so much that I didn't think I could do it.

"I can do it," I said, swallowing the nerves. "What do you think? We try it?"

"Hmm…" Natalie chewed on her nail for a moment, then hid her face in her hands and let out a laugh. "How have you got me considering standing up in front of six hundred people? That's like my worst nightmare, Gala."

"We will be great!" I poked her in the side. "You will be cool as a cucumber."

"I think it's much more likely that I'll shake like a jelly." Natalie laughed and swatted my hand away. "OK, OK. Let's do it. It's worth a try."

Twenty-six

We worked on the story all week. First we talked about what we wanted to say, and then Natalie found all the right words to say it with. My job was to learn them off by heart, and it wasn't easy. I typed them out on my phone and read them between classes and before bed. I recited them while I walked the dogs and took my bath. Once I had them memorized, I practised the ones that were trickier to pronounce over and over until they looked and sounded exactly right. I rehearsed so much that when I flossed at night I found lots of little words like *and* or *but* trapped between my teeth.

When Thursday came, I felt nervous but ready to stand up in assembly the next morning and tell the story we'd put together. I used our last detention to quickly do my Maths homework, then turned to a fresh page in the back of my English jotter and began writing it out to make sure I had it memorized. I wanted everything to go perfectly.

"Eilidh Chisholm!" Mr Rossi's voice was so loud it made everyone in detention jump. "You know you're not ~~~~~~ to have phones in here."

Eilidh C had joined us in detention again, this time for

talking during a German test. She mumbled some pale pink excuse but everyone could see her holding her phone under the desk. Mr Rossi walked over to her and held out his hand. She sighed and passed the phone to him.

"That's the second time I've warned you about this," he said. "Once more and I'll see you back in here on Monday."

Eilidh slumped back in her chair and said something under her breath. The word was too quiet for anyone to hear, and it slid quickly down her clothes and on to the pile of words heaped on the carpet. When I leaned forward to try to read what it said, my breath caught in my throat. It was a swear word in thin, curvy letters that sloped to the right, and it was the colour of red wine.

My heart started to pound as things slid into place. The trail of words that Natalie and I had followed last week hadn't been leading away from this classroom. It should have led us straight to it.

Because it had come from Eilidh C.

Eilidh C wrote the poems.

I nudged Natalie and nodded towards the word on the floor. It took her ages to spot it because there were already so many there, but when she did she flinched backwards like she'd been burned. I was so shocked that all I could do was stare. For months I had sat beside Eilidh C in classes, swapped crisps or chewing gum with her at break times, once let her copy my Graphic Communication homework when she'd forgotten to do hers. I'd thought she was my friend.

When the bell rang, Eilidh C swung her bag over her shoulder, went to get her phone back from Mr Rossi, and quickly left the classroom. Words were still swirling round my head, but I grabbed my bag and hurried out after her.

"It was you!" I wanted to shout but I was still in shock. Instead my words came out shaky and pale blue. "You wrote the poems."

Eilidh spun round. "What? No, I didn't."

She was lying. I could tell from the ways her words changed, becoming thinner and lighter in colour. I'd seen them do that in class when she told teachers that she really *had* done her homework, but had left it on the kitchen table.

"Yes, you wrote them," I insisted. "The poems had your words. Lots of them."

"I don't know what you're talking about, Gala." She looked at Natalie, who had run to catch up with us and was pulling something out of her schoolbag. "Did *she* tell you that? Because it's not true."

Natalie passed me the piece of the poem, then held out the word that had fallen on the floor in detention. I thrust them both at Eilidh.

"See? They are the same!"

Eilidh rolled her eyes. "You're being ridiculous. Can I go now? I've got stuff going on, you know. I don't have time to listen to this."

She pushed the door open but I wasn't going to let her deny it now that we had evidence. I followed her downstairs, insisting over and over that it was her. With each step, the shape of my words became firmer, their colours changing from unsure blues to a firm, vivid cerise. As we reached the back door, Eilidh whirled round and threw her hands up.

"Fine! It was me," she snapped. "I hated your stupid poems. I wanted them to stop."

Her words were large now but the colour was that familiar purplish red. This was a side of Eilidh that I hadn't seen before. An anger she never showed.

"Why?" I asked her.

"Because you wrote one for practically *everyone* in our year and not for me!" Eilidh shouted. "I knew it was you and Natalie sending them because I saw you picking up words in Chemistry and putting them in your pocket. After that, I kept waiting to get a poem, but you wrote to everybody who had the tiniest little problem and not to me. You were supposed to be my friend too, Gala."

Her eyes were shiny with anger. It had never occurred to me to ask Natalie about writing a poem for Eilidh C. Mostly because she kept saying they were weird and creepy but also because I wouldn't have known what to write one about. She could be cutting sometimes but she was always upbeat. Always talking.

"What problem do you have?"

I cringed when I said it because it sounded so blunt, but I didn't know how else to ask. Eilidh made a scoffing sound, but her lip was starting to tremble.

"My mum's not well." Her words came out wobbly, the colour dipping suddenly from deep red to pink. "She hasn't been well all year. And she's getting worse."

Her eyes teared up, and she turned away. I looked at Natalie. She shook her head to say she hadn't known, either.

"I am sorry," I said. "We didn't know. You did not say."

"Yes, I did!" said Eilidh, sniffing. "I talked to you about it in Art one day, remember? I said my mum had to go to Aberdeen for her treatment so I was staying with my gran for a few days."

I didn't remember that at all. Maybe I'd missed what Eilidh was saying, or maybe it got lost with all the other words that fell from her mouth. Sometimes she spoke so fast it was hard to tell where one topic ended and the next began.

"No… I am sorry," I said again, hoping she could tell from the deep blue colour that I really meant it.

"People always say they're sorry. That's *all* they say." Eilidh's words were turning red again. "I try to talk about it, and they say that's sad or such a shame, and then they change the subject. Nobody wants to talk about it. Nobody really cares."

I didn't get it. Eilidh C was so confident. She had so many friends, and all she did was talk. She talked all through classes and in the middle of games in PE and while we were doing tests. Teachers were always telling her off about it, and yet she couldn't stop. There were lots of times since I'd moved here that I'd watched the stream of words pouring from her mouth and felt jealous. I missed being able to do that, the way I used to with my friends.

But all that talking clearly didn't mean she could always say what she wanted to. It didn't mean she felt like anyone was listening. I knew what that was like.

Before I could work out how to say any of that, Eilidh C dabbed her eyes with the backs of her hands and sniffed. When she looked up, the sadness in her expression was gone.

"You can tell Mr Watson about this, but I'll deny it." She crossed her arms and smirked. "He plays golf with my dad, and I'll tell him you're trying to get me into trouble because I reported you. So don't even bother."

While I fumbled around, trying to put together a reply, she pushed open the door and ran outside, her ponytail swinging behind her. I caught the door but didn't run after her, and she didn't look back.

"I can't believe it." I said it in Catalan, more to myself than Natalie.

The words whipped out of the door and blew away on the breeze. Eilidh had never seemed keen on our poems but I'd never have guessed it was because she was jealous. I definitely couldn't have imagined she'd do something like this. She wasn't the person I thought she was at all.

Natalie was already kneeling down and picking up Eilidh's words. I checked that no teachers were coming, then tried to do the same, thinking we could patch the sentences back together and take them to Mr Watson. But it was hopeless – some of the words had blown away when she pushed the door open, and others were lost beneath all the other words littering the floor.

"What do you think?" I asked Natalie. "We tell Mr Watson?"

Natalie shook her head. Eilidh was right – we had no proof, and without it he would definitely take her side over ours.

"Let's do the story like we planned." She looked down at the words in her hand. "Actually, I think there are a couple of small things I might like to change. Do you think you'd have time to learn them by tomorrow?"

I told her I'd do my best. This story was our one shot at getting people to understand, but it wasn't only about proving ourselves innocent any more. It was about us and what we wanted to say.

So tomorrow we would stand up and say it.

Twenty-seven

The next morning, I woke up with words spinning round my head and nerves swirling in my stomach. I felt too anxious to eat breakfast, too sick to even speak. Papa kept putting his hand on my forehead to check if I had a fever, and he asked me twice if I wanted to stay off. The temptation to say yes and hide under my duvet all day was strong, but somehow I managed to shake my head and say I'd go to school. Natalie and I had worked really hard on our project. Even if everyone still hated us at the end of it, we had to try.

By the time we took our seats in assembly, I was so nervous I thought I might actually throw up. Beside me, Natalie kept picking at the skin around her fingernails, and her knee was bouncing up and down. I could barely follow what Mr Watson was saying. When he reached the end of his list of updates and wished everyone a nice weekend, I threw my hand into the air and stood up. Hundreds of faces turned to look at me. I felt mine turn bright red.

"Excuse me," I said. "Natalie and me, we have something to say."

Mr Watson blinked. "Here? Assembly is over, Gala.

You can…"

But I was already walking up to the stage, Natalie right behind me. My jelly legs tripped on the first step, but I kept going. I stood on the stage and looked out at the audience. Everyone in the school was there, hundreds of pupils and dozens of teachers. Most of the first-year faces were unfriendly – Craig and Abigail were sneering, and Eilidh C was scowling so hard it looked like she might hurt herself. Some of the teachers were whispering to each other, and Ryan was looking at me with a bewildered, worried expression.

But then I caught Eilidh O's eye, and she gave me an encouraging, if confused, smile. Somehow that gave me the strength to say the words I'd practised over and over all week. We put our schoolbags down on the stage, and I stepped towards Mr Watson.

"We have a story to tell."

"Gala, I really don't know if now is the time…" Mr Watson said, but Miss Shah interrupted him.

"Go on, Gala," she said, taking a step forward. "We're listening."

"OK." I swallowed. "Um, can we turn off the light, please?"

Some people laughed, and some rolled their eyes, but after a beat Ryan got up and flipped the switch. It was a dull, overcast morning, and the grey blinds had been pulled over the windows, probably to stop us from people-watching instead of listening to Mr Watson, so the room was cast into near-darkness. As Natalie stepped to the front of the stage, I crouched down and unzipped our backpacks. Inside mine was the galaxy lamp from my bedroom and a battery pack, which I set on the floor and turned on. I spun it until it shone straight on Natalie, bathing her in a slowly shifting galaxy of blue and purple stars.

Some people in the crowd were murmuring now. We had practised this for hours and hours this week but, for one horrible moment, my mind went totally blank, and I forgot every single word that I'd memorized. But I took a deep breath, waited for them to come back to me, and then started to speak.

"There was once a girl who lived in a snow globe," I said, making my words clear and large and loud, even though I felt small with so many people watching me. "But instead of snowflakes she was surrounded by words."

I dipped my hand into Natalie's bag, which was filled with thousands upon thousands of words. I took a fistful and threw them in the air. They rose up, then fell round Natalie like snowflakes, each one glittering in the sparkling lights of the galaxy lamp. As I scattered a second handful, Natalie spun slowly round. There were words in her hair, caught on her clothes, trapped behind her ears and stuck to her hands. She reached out to catch one and –

"That's enough!" Mr Watson stormed back across the stage. "I've already spoken to you two about this. Turn the lights back on and…"

"Wait!" Ryan was jogging down the aisle of the hall. "Let's hear them out."

Mr Watson looked down at him. His nostrils flared. "Mr Young, I've told Gala multiple times that I wanted no more word collecting."

"I know, I know, and they'll have to face the ∼∼∼∼∼. But they've already done it now." Ryan looked at me and then back to the head teacher. “Let them say their piece. Please, David.”

Miss Shah got up to speak to the head teacher too, and a couple of older kids in the audience shouted out, “Go on, sir.” They probably just wanted to avoid their next class for a little longer, but I was grateful to them anyway. Eventually Mr Watson sighed and looked at me and Natalie.

“Fine then,” he said, his words dark grey. “But come and see me afterwards.”

Natalie and I nodded. We waited for silence to settle again, and then I reached into my bag for another handful of words. Before school began this morning, we’d gone to the big bins behind the PE department and filled Natalie’s backpack to the brim with yesterday’s discarded words. We had enough to perform the whole story a few times over.

“There was once a girl who lived in a snow globe,” I said again. “But instead of snowflakes she was surrounded by words.”

This time, when I flung the words into the air, I paused for a moment to watch them flutter down to the floor before carrying on. Natalie looked so peaceful, spinning quietly in the word drift. Someone in the hall whispered something, and another person shushed them, then the room fell completely silent. Everyone was listening.

“The girl loved words. She had so many things she wanted to say with them. But, behind the thick glass of the snow globe, no one could hear her.” Natalie mimed banging on the inside of the dome. “It could be lonely in the globe. Sometimes it felt like she was stuck in a storm that no one else could see.”

When I got to the part about a storm, I tossed another handful of words and Natalie spun in fast, dizzying circles. When we had practised this at home, it looked silly, but here in her shimmering blue and purple spotlight, with hundreds of words twirling round her … it was sort of perfect.

"All day, the girl watched people pass by the globe. Soon she began to notice things."

My heart was still going at a hundred kilometres an hour, so I took a deep breath and paused. Natalie sat cross-legged on the floor and stared calmly out at our audience. Her jitters seemed to have vanished now. She seemed entirely still and serene.

"She saw that some people might talk a lot, but they couldn't say the things they really wanted to say. Many felt that no one could hear them, like she did. And, when she looked far, far into the distance, she saw there were other people in globes too. Hundreds and hundreds of them."

Moving on to her knees, Natalie reached out her hands and began pulling the words towards her in sweeping motions.

"The girl made a plan. She had always worried that people thought she didn't want to leave her globe, that she had no interest in the world outside or the people there. But that wasn't true. Sometimes she was happy where she was, but other times she had things to say, and she wished people could hear them. So she started collecting words and pressing them to the glass for those on the outside to read."

My mouth was getting tired from so much talking, so I took another deep breath and licked my lips while

Natalie moved the words around, the way she did when we were making poems. She gently picked one up with her thumb and forefinger and lifted it into the air. I moved the lamp round so that the light was pointing right at it. It cast a shadow against the wall that read ***hope***.

"The girl used the words to say the things she wanted to say, the things she thought people might like to hear. She wanted other people to know that they weren't alone, even if it felt that way sometimes. She only ever said good things, never bad. Even so, some people misunderstood her messages and turned away. But others understood her words and smiled. And that made her feel heard."

One by one, Natalie held other words up to the lamp. ***Fear. Change. Family. Alone. Love. Future. Listen.*** She let the final one drop from her fingers and looked up, frowning slightly. She reached out and brushed her fingers in an arc as if she was touching the inside of the globe.

"After some time, the girl noticed something. The words had created a tiny crack in the glass surrounding her. Seeing that, she knew that one day the globe would break open, and she would be able to leave if she wanted to."

I twisted the lamp again so the lights shone over Natalie and lit up her face. There were three words stuck to her cheeks and they glistened like tears. She brushed them off, and I took another deep breath before finishing our story.

"The girl didn't want to change or become someone else. She just wanted to step outside and be heard sometimes. The words were her way to do that."

I looked out at the audience. More than 600 people, all listening to what I was saying.

"Her way with words had become her way to the world."

I turned the lamp off. For a moment we were in near darkness, near silence, and it seemed to stretch on forever. But then one of the teachers turned the lights back on, and someone started clapping. I looked round and my heart skipped: the person applauding was Craig. It wasn't a joking, sarcastic clap – it looked like he actually meant it.

He was followed quickly by Ryan and Miss Shah, and then Eilidh O and Frankie. A few more people joined in, and soon the whole hall was clapping. I held out my hand to Natalie, and she got to her feet. She was half grinning, like she couldn't believe what she was seeing or hearing. I couldn't, either – even Mr Watson joined in the applause, though the frown didn't fade from his face. We'd done it. Natalie and I had really done it.

So, with our hands joined and thousands of words scattered at our feet, we stepped forward and took a bow.

Twenty-eight

Unfortunately, all the applause didn't get us out of trouble. Mr Watson gave us each another full week of detention for 'stealing' words from the bin. He also told us to stay behind after the end of assembly to pick up all the words that we'd thrown over the stage, but we'd planned on doing that anyway. As everyone trailed out of the hall, Ryan and Miss Shah came up to the stage to talk to us.

"That was really brave, what you did up there," said Miss Shah, smiling at me. "I'm so impressed with both of you."

"It was brilliant." Ryan's words were a shiny purple. "I'm really proud of you, Gala."

Even though we were in school and he was supposed to be Mr Young here, I stood on my tiptoes and threw my arms round Ryan. "I don't want to move back to Cadaqués!"

The words slipped out without my permission, without my even knowing they were waiting to escape. Ryan leaned back to look at me. "What?"

"I heard you and Papa talking about it after we dropped Iaia off at the airport," I said in Catalan. "But I don't want to go back there any more. We're a family. I want us all to be together."

Ryan blinked at me. For one horrifying second I thought he might cry – I'd seen Ryan cry twice, both times at dogs dying in films, and it sounded like he'd swallowed a whistle – but then he laughed and pulled me into a big hug again.

"Don't worry. Your dad and I aren't going to make any more decisions without you," he said, his words now a warm shade of caramel. "We just want you to be happy."

"I am happy here." This time I spoke in English, and my words came out in sunshine yellow to show I really meant them. "I mean, there is no Iaia. No churros. Not such good weather. But we have Celine and Dion, and we have you. And that is what we need most."

That made Ryan get that oh-no-a-fictional-dog-is-about-to-die look again. He quickly glanced down at his trainers, which were now covered in words from our performance, muttered something about borrowing a broom from the janitor and hurried off. He came back a few minutes later with dustpans and brushes for us to sweep the stage and gave us both congratulatory high fives before he went to the gym to teach his next class.

Natalie and I took our time, making sure we swept every single word from the stage, then chose the long route back to the storage cupboard to return the dustpans and brushes. We had Maths next, and I wanted to put off going as long as possible. Even though everyone had clapped for us, I still wasn't sure if the kids in our class would believe our story. We might have made things even worse for ourselves.

But, either way, I was proud of us. When I came to Scotland three months ago, I could never have done something like I did today. If anyone had asked me to try,

I would have refused. There were a few times this morning when the sentences had flowed out of my mouth as easily as if they were my first language, the colours bright and the shapes of the letters clear and fluid. Even if I still had lots to learn, English was starting to feel like it was mine too.

When we pushed open the door to the classroom, everyone turned to stare – even Mr Henderson stopped mid-explanation of Pythagoras' theorem to look at us. My whole body froze but then Craig leaned back in his chair and linked his hands behind his head.

"Your story was pretty good. That thing where you threw up the words like they were snowflakes – that was clever."

"Yeah," Ben Dupont said in cobalt blue. "And the bit where you held the words up to the light. I liked that."

"It was very nice, Gala," said Mr Henderson, smiling. I think it might have been the first time I ever saw him smile. "Now, if we could all get back to..."

"Was it really not you who wrote those weird messages to me and Eilidh Chisholm and the others then?" Abigail asked loudly.

Everyone was quiet. I looked at Natalie. Now that we knew who'd really left the poems, people might finally believe that we were innocent. We might even get an apology from some of the people who'd said such mean things about us. But I thought about Eilidh C, worried about her mum, feeling as if no one was listening. I didn't want to make things harder for her. So, when Natalie shook her head, I did the same.

"No, it was not," I said, turning to Abigail. "Maybe we never know who did it."

"Weird." Abigail shrugged. "Well, sorry I blamed you."

She looked at me as she said it, then gave Natalie something that was almost like a smile. Natalie couldn't have looked more shocked if Abigail had turned into a unicorn and started singing a Taylor Swift song.

Mr Henderson cleared his throat and started going on about Maths again, so I hurried across the room and took my seat beside Eilidh O. When he'd finished explaining the exercises, and we'd all settled down to work, she leaned towards me.

"It was Eilidh C, wasn't it?" she whispered, so quietly that I had to read the words that fell on to her textbook. "She's the one who sent those mean poems."

I blinked at her. "You knew all the time?"

Eilidh O shook her head. "No! I figured it out earlier. She was so quiet walking back from assembly. She didn't say a single word the whole way, and you know that's not like her." She leaned closer. "If you want to go to Mr Watson, I'll back you up. It's not fair that you took the blame for what she did."

"It is OK." I searched for a phrase that Ryan liked to use. "She has a lot in her bowl."

"A lot on her plate, you mean?" Eilidh O smiled. "Yeah, I know. That doesn't make it OK, though. It was bullying, what she did."

It was, and there was never an excuse for that. But I still wanted to give Eilidh C a chance. I shook my head, and Eilidh O said OK and passed me her milk-carton pencil case. I picked out a pen decorated with llamas in bow ties, then tried to focus on the language of numbers.

When the bell rang for break, Eilidh C was waiting outside our classroom. Her face was pale behind her freckles, and she was nervously rubbing her right foot against the back of her other leg.

"I'm sorry about the poems," she said, blurting out the words so fast they were almost stuck together. "It was really stupid."

"And it was bullying." Eilidh O's words were as cold and sharp as icicles. "Don't forget that part."

"Yeah, I know. I'm sorry. I don't know what I was thinking. I just felt so... It doesn't matter. I shouldn't have done it." Eilidh C looked at her feet. "I'm going to go to Mr Watson now and tell him it was me. But can you please, *please* not tell anyone else? I don't want everyone to hate me."

"Like they hate us for the last weeks?" I said hotly. Natalie put her arm on my sleeve and squeezed it. I let out a breath. "OK. We say nothing."

"Thank you, Gala. And you, Natalie. I really am sorry." When Eilidh C looked up, some of the colour had come back to her cheeks. She turned to Eilidh O. "I'll meet you upstairs with Frankie and the others afterwards?"

"Nah, that's OK." Eilidh O gave a tight smile that didn't reach her eyes. "I'll see you in French."

Her words were a cool violet colour now and clipped around the edges. Eilidh C looked hurt, but she nodded. She walked away from us quickly, not looking back before she turned the corner towards reception and the head teacher's office. Once she was gone, Eilidh O cleared her throat and gave Natalie a nervous smile.

"I was wondering... Maybe I could have lunch with you

two today?" she asked us. "I think I've had enough of being one half of a pair."

I looked at Natalie. Her face was tense for a moment. We were so used to spending lunchtimes just the two of us, and adding a new person to the mix was a big change. But then a small smile broke through, and she nodded – I was so pleased I clapped my hands like a seal. My friends both laughed, and the three of us walked together to our next class.

Twenty-nine

The sky cleared up while Natalie, Eilidh and I were having lunch together, and by the afternoon the weather was bright and sunny. Eilidh O had tap-dancing classes in Inverness on Fridays but Natalie came with me after school to walk the dogs. She hadn't been able to speak much at lunch with Eilidh there – it would take a while for her to feel comfortable enough to do that – so the walk down the hill to our house was the first time we'd been able to really talk since our performance.

"I can't believe we did it," she said. "You were so good! You sounded perfect."

"Really?" My face broke into a big grin at that. "I think maybe I have messed up some words."

"Not at all. But, even if you did, who cares? Everyone could understand you, and you said what we wanted to say. That's the most important thing."

"I am proud of you too," I said, bumping my arm against hers. "You act very well. Sometimes, watching you, I almost forgot to keep speaking."

Natalie laughed. "Thanks. I always liked the idea of acting, you know." She stopped to pick up a word that was caught on a daisy, a pale yellow *world*. "Maybe I'll join the drama club one day. Eilidh O is in it, isn't she? You should come too!"

I said I'd think about it. I was also considering joining the netball team and maybe trying out for the girls' football team after the summer holidays, so I wasn't sure I'd have time. I missed playing sports and being part of a team. Ryan was going to be so excited. I couldn't wait to tell him.

"Do you think Eilidh C really told Mr Watson the truth?" Natalie asked me.

"Yes, I believe so."

Her words had been clear and bold when she told us that, so it didn't seem as if she was lying. Part of me had been hoping the head teacher would come and find us at lunchtime and give a grovelling apology for not believing us, but of course that hadn't happened. It wasn't important, though. We'd said what we wanted to say, and people had listened. That was what counted.

I pushed open the door to our house and shouted a big green hello. The dogs raced through the hallway to greet me, as always. When Dion saw Natalie, he got so excited he jumped up and bumped his head on the lampshade. Papa followed them out, laughing. He said hello to Natalie and scooped up Celine, who was trying to start a fight with Ryan's running shoes.

"Ryan told me about your performance at school today," Papa said, speaking in English so Natalie could understand. His words were peach-coloured and he was smiling from ear to ear. "It sounded excellent. I wish I had been there to see it."

"Natalie was amazing," I said. "Like a real actor."

"It's *actress* for women," Papa told me, but Natalie and I both shook our heads.

"Actor is OK too. Some people think it is better," I said.

Miss Shah had taught me that last week, while we were talking about our favourite films.

Papa looked surprised but then he laughed and ruffled my hair. "See? You know more than me already."

We went into the kitchen, and he made us a snack of chocolate sandwiches. Natalie's schoolbag was still half full of the words we'd taken from the bin, and we went through them while we ate, looking for interesting ones. I ran upstairs to get my biscuit tin to save the ones I liked best.

"I still do not know what to do with them," I said. "I think not poems. Poems are your thing."

Papa looked up from his computer. "What about that notebook Natalie gave you for your birthday? You could put them in there."

That gave me an idea. Cramming the last of my sandwich into my mouth, I dashed up to my bedroom again and came back with the notebook.

"I can make a book like you are making for Ava!" I said in bright orange. "Not first words, of course, but ones that I like or want to remember."

Natalie grinned and held up a finger to tell me to wait. She took one word from my biscuit tin, rummaged around in her bag for some others and laid them out on the table. They said **The** Dictionary of Gala. I laughed and clapped my hands.

"Yes! I love it."

I picked up the title and rearranged it on the first page.

I could put all sorts of words in there, in English and Catalan and Spanish and any other languages that I might learn in the future too. An A to Z of the words that made up my world.

Natalie and I were still arranging the first page – starting with *avocado*, one of my favourite foods, and **aixopluc**, the Catalan word for a shelter from the rain – when Ryan got back from netball practice. He arrived carrying three huge portions of fish and chips wrapped in newspaper.

"I didn't feel like cooking," he explained, setting everything down on the worktop.

"You never do any cooking," said Papa, laughing. "I think you survived on cereal and beans on toast before we moved in."

Ryan swatted at him with a tea towel. "OK, fine, I just wanted chips. Besides, it's such a nice evening out. How about we take these down to the Point? Do you want to come too, Natalie? There's enough for four."

Natalie texted her mum to ask, and once she'd got the OK we all headed out with Celine and Dion.

When we got to the lighthouse, we unclipped the dogs, and they bolted down the beach, barking happily. We followed behind them, then Papa found an old Frisbee lying under a bench, and we threw it for a very overexcited Dion. After a while, Ryan went to stop Celine from pushing over a bin, and Natalie wandered towards the golf course, looking for words, so it was only Papa and me left playing.

"Why didn't you tell me you were planning on doing a performance at school?" he asked, switching to Catalan now we were alone.

I shrugged. "It's not like it was a full play, Papa. It was just a story we wrote to explain why we made the poems."

"Still, I could have helped you practise."

Papa swung his arm back, then flung the Frisbee across the beach. Dion gave a delighted yelp and went racing after it for the hundredth time, spraying us both with sand.

"I'm proud of you, Gala. You've been working so hard."

"Well, we had to prove our innocence," I said, making my words breathy and a dramatic black as if I was on a TV show.

"I'm glad you did. And I'm sorry again that I didn't believe you right away." He put his arm round me. "You know I'm always on your side, bug. No matter what."

I leaned my head against his shoulder. "I'm always on yours too. Unless we're playing video games. Then it's every person for themself."

Papa shook his head and laughed. The Frisbee had gone into the water, and Dion was splashing around, trying to find it. "Only two weeks until the Easter holidays now. Are you looking forward to going home?"

"Yes!"

Of course I was. Even after less than a week apart, I couldn't wait to see Iaia again. I couldn't wait to eat her torrijas for Easter and dance round the kitchen to pop songs with her. I couldn't wait to see Pau and Mariam and Laia, to get churros from our favourite spot and play ping-pong in the park. I couldn't wait to feel the sunshine on my skin and the waves round my ankles.

"But…" I paused and took in the quiet sweep of the beach, the green of the hills in the distance, the vast open sky above me. I looked at Ryan and the dogs and Natalie, thought about Eilidh O and strawberry tarts and speeding down those water slides on my birthday. "But I'll be happy to *come* home too."

A big smile broke over Papa's face. He linked his other arm round me and kissed the top of my head. We had two homes now. Two countries and three whole languages we could call our own. We were lucky.

By now, Celine had got bored of the bin and was chasing after Dion for the wet Frisbee. Natalie and Ryan came running behind her, both out of breath and laughing, and we all sat down to eat on the sand. Having dinner this early still seemed strange to me, but my stomach rumbled gratefully when Ryan handed me and Natalie our portion.

The fish and chips were warm and delicious – another thing that I'd added to my list of things I liked best about living here. Miss Shah told me that the fried-fish part of the recipe originally came from Jewish immigrants from Spain and Portugal, hundreds of years ago now. I'd liked hearing that. That something so typically British had been partly created by people a bit like me.

As Natalie and I had a battle over an extra-large chip with our little wooden forks, my eye caught something moving in the sea – a quick flash of grey in the waves, and then another and another.

"Look!" I shouted. "The dolphins!"

I put down my food and ran to the edge of the water. There were five or six of them leaping in and out of the waves a few metres from the shoreline. Other people began coming closer, pointing and taking out their phones. It was as if the dolphins knew we'd been waiting for them.

"So they *are* real!" I said, turning to Ryan.

"Of course they're real," he said, his words coming out a deep plum colour as he pretended to be offended. "Did you think I was making them up?"

Papa laughed. "I have to admit, I was starting to have my doubts too."

I reached for my phone – I wanted to get proof they actually existed to show Iaia – then let my hand drop. There would be other chances to take photos. Instead I stood and simply watched the dolphins showing off. Papa and Ryan stood beside me, their arms round each other, and Celine and Dion splashed in the waves. I turned to Natalie with a huge smile.

"I can't believe we see them! Finally!"

She grinned and held out her hand. There was one word in her palm: **perfect**, in my favourite shade of raspberry pink. And this moment was exactly that.

I took the word and put it in my pocket. It would be another entry for my dictionary when I got home. But, for now, I turned back to the water and watched the dolphins leaping and playing in the evening sun, all heading towards the glittering horizon in the distance.

Read on for an extract from

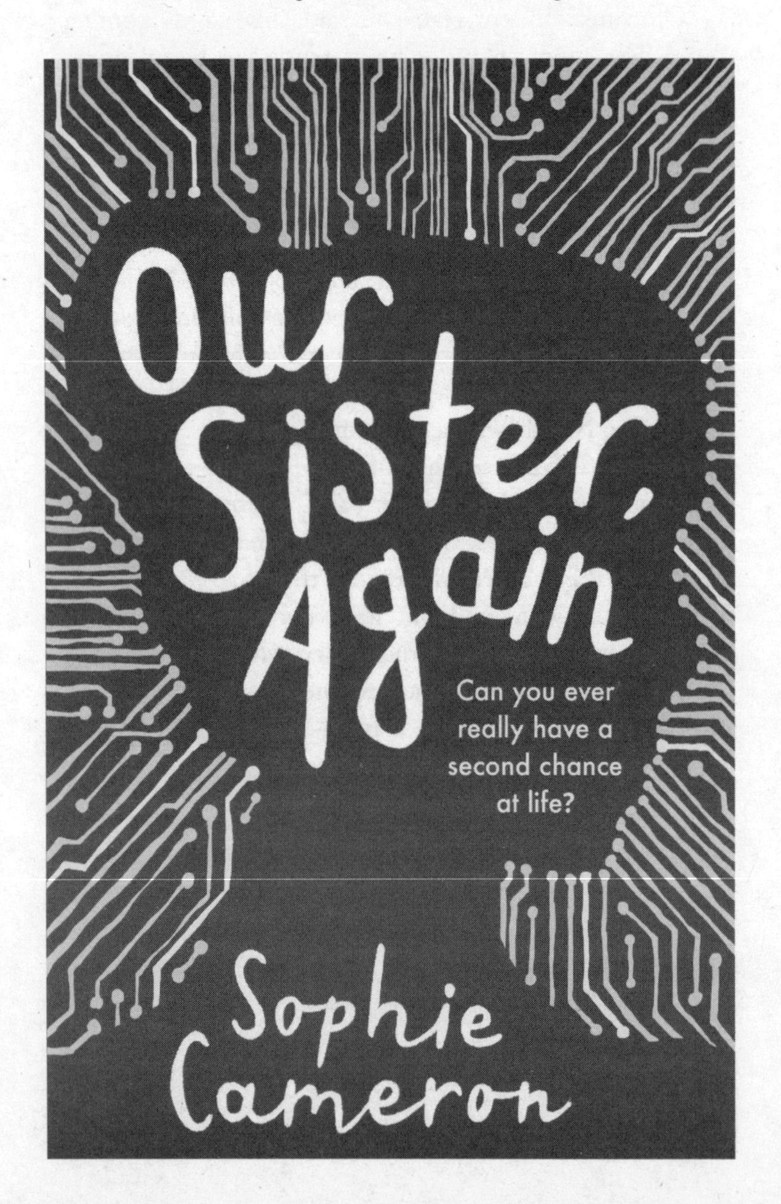

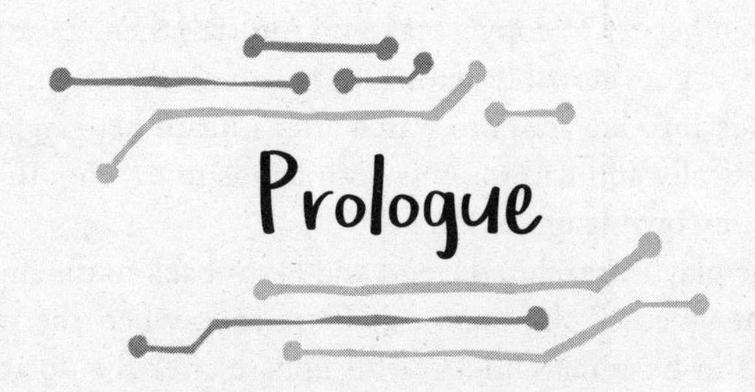

Prologue

I'm watching the videos again. I'm supposed to be doing my German homework, but twenty minutes ago I picked up my phone to find the word for watermelon, got distracted by a notification from the Sekkon app, and now I'm watching my sister serenade our cat.

On the screen, Flora sits cross-legged on her bed, singing into a hairbrush. When she gets to the chorus, she holds the pretend mic out to Sìth. The cat lets out a long meow that's so perfectly in tune with the song that Flora jumps back and falls off the bed. The video has over twenty thousand views, 132 comments. I can see a few of them at the bottom of the screen.

Too cute!

Omg your cat is channelling Ariana Grande

Rest in peace, Flora. We miss you.

The video ends and rolls on to the next one, then the next. There are 389 videos on Flora's Sekkon account. I've seen them all a million times before, but I keep watching anyway. I watch Flora unbox an American snack pack that a friend sent for her birthday and dance to a K-pop song with three girls from her swim team.

I watch her try to copy a make-up tutorial, then crack up when it goes horribly wrong. (That one's my favourite. I snuck into her room to watch after I heard her giggling hysterically and had to press both hands to my mouth to stifle my own laughter.)

The playlist reaches the end and loops back to the most recent videos – the ones that Flora took when she was bored in hospital, and a tearful update after the doctors told us there was nothing more they could do. I skip those. I like seeing Flora laughing and joking around, being silly and carefree. That's the way I want to remember her: my loud, funny, bossy big sister.

Mum comes into the kitchen carrying a stack of mugs and plates. I put my phone face down on the table and turn back to my German grammar exercises. Bringing up Flora around my parents is always a risk. Some days we end up laughing about happy times or funny things she used to say, but on others it plunges them into darkness. I can tell from the cloudy look in her eyes as Mum walks to the sink that today is one of the bad days.

"Do you need a hand, Mum? I can wash those up, if you like."

"Hmm?" Mum looks round at me. Her voice sounds faraway, like she's talking from the bottom of a very deep pit. "Oh. No thanks, Isla, it's fine. You carry on with your homework."

She falls silent as she washes the dishes, lost in her memories. In the living room, Dad is watching an interior design show while my little sister Ùna lies on the carpet, reading. Everything looks quiet and calm but the atmosphere is heavy as a storm. Great big thunder clouds of grief rolled over our house when Flora died. A year and a half later, they still haven't cleared.

Of course I knew I'd miss her. But I didn't know how much, or that I'd even miss the way she hogged the bathroom and snapped at me for borrowing her pens. I also hadn't expected how much I'd miss Mum and Dad. That sounds strange, since they're still here in the house with me, but they're not the same. Especially Mum. She doesn't sing along to the radio or quote old TV shows like she used to. It feels like forever since I saw her smile – her real smile, not a quick turn-up of the lips.

Dad is a little better. He has his down days but lately he's started cracking his terrible jokes and puns again. Hearing them is like a ray of sunlight slipping through the dark clouds, even if they still make me groan. He keeps suggesting that we sort out the things in Flora's bedroom for charity shops, or that we finally scatter her ashes, but Mum always finds an excuse not to. Those things are all we have left of Flora.

She's not ready to say goodbye yet.

And that means none of us can.

Mum leaves the plates and cups to dry and goes back to the living room. When I pick up my phone again, an advert has popped up on the screen.

HOMEWARD HEALING

A free online support group for those struggling with bereavement.
Join us and take a brave step towards a happier future.

Find out more

Sekkon is full of ads but I've never seen one like this before. They usually show me football boots or cat T-shirts, whatever I've searched for recently. My friend Murdo's dad is always going on about how big tech companies are tracking us and selling our personal information to advertisers. This feels different, though – it's almost like they've read my mind.

I click on the link. It takes me to a really basic website with a short description about how the group is open to anyone who has lost a loved one, and a form to enter your contact details. Maybe this is what Mum needs. We live on a tiny island in the Outer Hebrides, just 163 inhabitants. There are no support groups like this nearby. We all did online sessions with a grief counsellor last year but Mum and Dad gave up on theirs pretty quickly. They said it was too expensive, and that it wasn't helping much either. A group would be good for them. They could meet other people who have lost a child. People who really know what they're going through.

In the living room, my parents' faces are lit up blue in the glow of the TV screen. Without asking their permission, I type Mum's name and email address into the form and click send. The thought of scattering Flora's ashes, boxing up her things … it makes me feel sick with sadness. But nothing is going to bring her back. We need to be brave and start taking steps forwards, like the ad says. Maybe this will be the first.

Acknowledgements

Thank you so much to everyone at Little Tiger for all their hard work on this book, especially my brilliant editors, Mattie Whitehead and Karelle Tobias, and Pip Johnson for making it look so gorgeous inside and out!

Thank you to my agent, Hellie Ogden, and to Grace Kavanagh, Dan Shapiro, Linda Freund and Andrew Critchley for their feedback on early drafts.

Thank you to my friends and family, especially to Naïa for the constant support, ideas and cups of tea when the words are flowing.

Moltes gràcies to the many Catalan teachers I've had over the years for sharing your wonderful language and helping inspire this story.

And a huge thank you, as always, to everyone – readers, authors, librarians, teachers, booksellers, bloggers – who has read and supported my books so far. I am so grateful, and I hope you enjoy this one too.

About the Author

Sophie Cameron is a YA and MG author from the Scottish Highlands. She studied French and Comparative Literature at the University of Edinburgh and has a Postgraduate Certificate in Creative Writing from Newcastle University. Her debut novel *Out of the Blue* was nominated for the Carnegie Medal 2019. She lives in Spain with her family.